Tantalizing Twink
A Collection of Gay Erotica fror

by
PJ Dominicis

(Writing as Peter Z Pan)
Previously published in
STARbooks Press Anthologies

ADULTS ONLY

PRINT EDITION

Copyright © 2016 by PJ Dominicis

This book is a work of fiction. The names, characters, places, and incidents are products of the writer's imagination or have been used fictitiously and are not to be construed as real. Any resemblance to persons, living or dead, actual events, locales or organizations is entirely coincidental.

All rights are reserved. No part of this book may be used or reproduced in any manner whatsoever without the written permission of the author.

Cover Photo by Peter Z Pan. Used with permission from copyright owner, Peter Zaragoza. The model is over 18 years of age, proof on file.

These stories originally appeared on the pages of STARbooks Press anthologies in the 90's.

While the words "boy," "girl," "young man," "youngster," "gal," "kid," "student," "guy," "son," "youth," "fella," and other such term are occasionally used in text, this work is generally about persons who are at least 18 years of age, unless otherwise noted.

First Edition.

Published by
PZP Enterprises
PO Box 8501
Fort Lauderdale, FL 33310

PREFACE

These stories are from a different time, so they may shock and/or offend modern-day, hyper sensitivities. They deal with delicate issues in an offbeat, whimsical, and sometimes perverse manner. I don't know if they have redeeming social value; however, I believe they sometimes transcend erotica into other genres. Some of them may even tug at your heart or, God forbid, open your mind.

If you are easily offended, then this book is <u>NOT</u> for you.

SWEET DREAMS

"Sweet dreams till sunbeams find you,
Sweet dreams that leave all worries behind you.
But in your dreams whatever they be,
Dream a little dream of me."
—Mama Cass

Dawn in the Miami Marina. Blissful silence, not a soul in sight. On the deck of the Caravaggio Amor, the waking sun's soothing rays bathed my naked body. This was a daily ritual for me. I stroked my fat cock thinking of *him*, as I did every morning. Only today was different. Today, I would breathe the same air as he. I erupted with a fury, my hot cum spurting on my face, chest, and stomach. *Today* was the day!

I knew who the kid was the minute I laid eyes on him: the bushy blond hair, the deep blue eyes, the cleft chin. It had to be him. Nathan Landis, the resident smart-ass kid on "OceanTrek," the only TV show I could actually sit through without falling asleep. Nathan was really the biggest reason I watched the show every Sunday night. There was just something about this eighteen-year-old kid that made my fat cock come to life. Now here he was, standing on my boat.

"OceanTrek" was shooting on location, on a small island between Miami and Bermuda. The producers had chartered my boat to take the actors to and from the set. Nathan had a late call that day, much to my delight, so he was my *only* passenger on that fateful trip.

"He needs to be on set five minutes ago!" whined the effeminate production assistant who escorted Nathan to the boat. "You take good care of our little star."

"Fuck off," I muttered as we shoved off.

There we were, just Nathan Landis and me on a picturesque, South Florida day. But things were not exactly the way I had fantasized. I stood *alone* at the wheel and Nathan sat quietly on the bow of the boat, looking out at the open sea. Not exactly a wet dream come true.

"Beautiful day, ain't it?" I blurted out, desperately trying to make small talk.

"It's too hot," Nathan shyly murmured, quite the contrast from the outgoing kid I was used to seeing on TV.

"It's summer in Miami, son," I said removing my T-shirt. "Why don't you take your shirt off?"

He looked at me as if I had asked him to take out his cock or something. "No, I can't," he stated adamantly.

"Why not?" I asked. "It's just you and me."

"I never take my shirt off in front of strangers," he said. "You see, I'm real skinny. I don't have the nice body you have." The last sentence slipped out, making him blush.

"I can fix that," I assured him. "Come here."

The kid did what he was told; he reluctantly stood next to me. I tried to make eye contact. However, as much as he tried, he could not take his gaze off my big, brawny body. He seemed fixated on my hairy chest, licking it with his hungry eyes.

"Hi, my name's Jack O'Brien," I said, as I vigorously shook his hand.

"Nathan, Nathan Landis," he uttered, his voice quivering.

"Well, nice to meet you, Nate," I said.

"Nathan," he corrected me with a bit of an ex-child star attitude.

"Whatever. But since we're no longer strangers, you can take your shirt off."

This brought a smile to the kid's face for the first time. "Okay, I guess," he said with a sheepish grin. Nathan lifted his T-shirt, revealing a beautiful callow torso, untouched by manhood. He had a lanky swimmer's build and small, pink nipples that just begged to be nibbled on.

I was about to wipe the drool from my chin when it happened. The boat's compass suddenly started going haywire and dark clouds appeared from nowhere. I had never before seen rain clouds assemble so rapidly.

Shit, we're in the Bermuda triangle! I thought. *We're right smack in the friggin' Bermuda triangle! This can't be happening!*

Gusts of wind and rain hit us as huge waves began to toss the boat.

"Jack…Jack, what's happening?!" screamed the kid. He held on to me, frightened out of his wits.

I couldn't answer; I was too busy trying to make sense of the situation myself, and trying to get control of the boat. The last thought that went through my head before passing out, was that of the Skipper and Gilligan spinning, spinning out of control.

We awoke on a sprawling white beach. Apparently, we had somehow been washed ashore. Nathan and I just looked at each other at a loss for words, not really knowing if we were dead or alive, or just having some horrid nightmare. There was not a cloud in the sky now. It was as if the storm had never occurred.

"Are you all right, son?" I inquired with genuine concern.

The kid nodded and then asked, "Are we alive, Jack?"

"Yeah, son. By some miracle of God, it looks like we're alive," I replied, caressing his long, blond hair.

After several hours of exploring, Nathan and I discovered we were on a deserted island. It was a beautiful tropical island too, with plenty of fruits on the trees and drinking water in the ponds. We soon came upon a large, crystal clear lagoon with stunning waterfalls all around. The water was a lovely shade of blue I had never before seen. It was breathtaking, to say the least.

"Wow, it's beautiful," sighed the kid.

"Yeah, it is, ain't it," I concurred. "Last one in's a rotten egg," I playfully bellowed as I quickly undressed.

"But I don't have swimming trunks!" whimpered the kid.

"Forget it, boy. C'mon. Let's skinny-dip." With that, I pulled down my pants and exposed my ten-inch dick to him.

It was obvious that he had never seen a cock that big before. He was absolutely transfixed by it. You could tell that he yearned to touch it, but did not dare. I was now completely naked. The kid's eyes were glued to my virile, teddy bear body. I then let out a hearty laugh when I noticed his gaze still focused on my man-meat.

"Sorta makes you think of a salami, don't it, son?"

The kid nodded in awe while I undressed him. First his T-shirt. His supple chest and arms were lean but well-defined, and he was smooth as a baby's bottom, except for the trace of a few hairs under his arms. I knelt and pulled down his pants and underpants. An amused smile took over my face at the sight of his peter. It was so damn cute! The puberty fairy had apparently gotten stuck in traffic on the way to his house. He was eighteen, yet only a few strands of blond hair surrounded his penis. It lay dormant upon his ripe, plump balls.

I rose as the kid stepped out of his pants. We looked at each other, smiled, and then ran buck-naked into the lagoon. Now, *our* lagoon.

After hours of frolicking in the water, I sent Nathan out to pick some fruit. In the meantime, I fished with a spear that I had made it out of a bamboo stick, using my trusty pocketknife. Nathan's Boy Scout training came in handy too; he effortlessly started a fire to fry the fish. Of course, my Zippo lighter didn't hurt. With our stomachs full, we dealt with the next problem at hand: finding shelter before dusk.

To complicate matters, an ominous looking storm was approaching. The heavy winds came first, followed by deafening thunder, blinding lightning, and ice-cold rain. We were two paper dolls caught in a furious tempest. A frightened Nathan began to cry, as panic began to set in.

"Look!" Nathan screamed, pointing to a small cave several feet away.

I grabbed him by the hand and made a run for it just as a bolt of lightning struck the very spot we had been standing on, barely missing us. We had lucked out. We had found a cozy little cave for me and my cub to hibernate in.

"I'm freezing," Nathan complained, literally shaking. The temperature seemed to have dropped fifty degrees.

"We have to get out of these wet clothes, son," I said, and then began to undress.

Nathan hesitated for a split second, then realized he had no other logical choice. He too got naked. I collected some twigs and branches that were strewn in the cave, quickly starting a bonfire by the entrance.

"I'm still cold," he complained.

"We have to share our body heat," I told him, sprawling on the ground by the fire. "Come here, son."

Nathan lay next to me, still shaking. Only, I didn't know if he was shaking from the cold or from what he knew was about to happen.

"Relax, son, it's okay," I said, trying to comfort him. "We have to share our body heat."

His skinny body went limp, surrendering to mine as I took him into my strong, manly arms. He felt so fucking good in my arms, like he belonged there. Before I could worry about his reaction to my fat hard-on prodding him, I felt *his* fledgling boner poking mine. He was as turned on as I was!

We gazed into each other's eyes, our faces just inches apart, our ardent breaths igniting each other.

"Do you feel any warmer, son?" I whispered.

"Oh yes!" he sighed. "I'm warm all over."

With that, the kid began to quiver. I was about to ask him if he was okay, when I felt the warmth of his seed gushing onto my stomach. After catching his breath, he looked as if he was about to say something and then thought better of it. Instead, his cheeks turned beet red as tears flooded his baby blues.

"What's wrong, son?"

"I'm so embarrassed," he confessed, weeping.

My only thought at that moment was to comfort him somehow. Without thinking, I held his head firmly in my hands and kissed him, kissed him hard.

The kid didn't even try to pull away. Instead, he greeted my ravenous tongue with his own, tasting everything my eager mouth had to offer. We were both in heat and there was no turning back now. Our makeshift lair was ablaze with passion.

I rolled on top of him and continued to feast upon his delicate face: his ripe lips, his waxy ears, his tangy neck. But I was insatiable! I wanted, I needed, *more*. I licked my way down his lithe, young body to his armpits. They were warm and musky. After lapping at his pits for a while, I proceeded to his tiny pink nipples. I nibbled on them hard, coming damn close to drawing blood. But the kid didn't seem to mind, he was lost in ecstasy.

I giddily kissed my way down his chest to his stomach, which was still wet and sticky from his premature ejaculation. The taste of cum filled my hungry mouth. I ate it up like a wild animal, feeding to survive. But this wasn't enough for me, I still needed more. I rubbed my face hard into his stomach until his white honey went up my nostrils, in my eyes, in my hair. I was drunk on it. My face was a milky white, just dripping with his cum.

After licking his tummy dry, I continued my descent to his prick. Much to my surprise, it was quite erect again.

Not yet, I thought.

I decided to save it for the main course. So, I started with a hearty appetizer instead: his plump, juicy balls. They were like butter, melting in my sultry mouth. I sucked the left one first, then the right one, then both at the same time. That's when I felt droplets trickling down my nose and lips. Licking my lips, I quickly realized the kid was oozing pre-cum. I couldn't stand it anymore. It was time for the entree.

The kid quivered as I took his cock in my mouth. My jaded taste buds came alive with this choice cut of veal. It was absolutely succulent.

I didn't want the kid to shoot another load yet, so I reluctantly left his throbbing pecker alone. Placing one hand under each supple cheek, I lifted his butt off the ground. I could now see his vestal, pink hole glistening with boy-juice. The aroma was intoxicating; sweet yet tangy, like a locker room after gym class. I nudged it with my nose, and then opened my mouth just in time to catch a droplet of his juice with my swift tongue. It was fucking delicious! His boy-pussy tasted as good as it smelled. I took a deep breath and dove in, eating him out in earnest.

That's when the guttural sounds caught my attention: groaning, moaning, grunting. Yes, they were emanating from the kid, but they were also coming from me. I was eating him out sloppily and loudly, like a pig at a trough. And I was loving every minute of it. I could tell the kid was about to bust his nut once more, and this time I wanted to gobble down every last drop of his jism, so I had him sit on my chest, with one leg on each side of my head.

"Grab me by the hair, Nate," I directed him. "Grab me by the hair and fuck my mouth like a wet twat, son!"

The kid took direction well. He rammed his cock down my throat and fucked my face like a twenty-dollar hustler on Biscayne Boulevard. Within seconds, I was swallowing globs of his spunk. I rolled on top of him then and kissed him hard, sharing his cum in our mouths.

My cock felt like it was about to explode. I needed relief fast! I threw his legs over my shoulders, spat into his pink hole, and then spat on my fat shaft. I shoved just the head into his tight virgin pussy, hesitating for a moment. This was going to hurt like a motherfucker. I remembered my first time, when Father McIntire butt-fucked me in the confessional. Hell, I took it and I survived. And Nathan would survive too. He had to. It was a rite of manhood!

"Brace yourself, son," I warned him tenderly. Then I ferociously rammed it into him with a savage fury.

I heard a loud *pop* as a streak of his cherry red blood sprayed my face. I licked my lips; tasting his cherry as I fucked him, fucked him on his back with his legs in the air like the little bitch that he was. He looked up at me with tears in his eyes, but I didn't care. I continued to ride him deep, ride him hard, ride him rough. Then I threw him on all fours and mounted him from behind like two dogs in heat. I humped him doggy-style, finally collapsing on top of him while continuing to pound his skinny, white ass.

I roared, shooting my load deep inside him. That's when I looked up and saw them for the first time. That's why the kid looked so frightened. There were dozens of huge, black natives standing around us, whacking their horse-dicks. One of them, the biggest one, hit me across the face with his massive phallus and I passed out!

I awoke to find myself tied to a totem pole of sorts, in a clearing deep in the woods. Several feet in front of me, the natives were gathered over my Nathan, who was tied spread-eagle to a bed made out of stone. A huge black snake squiggled on the kid's naked body. It did this almost sensuously, like it was making love to him. The natives stood over Nathan, chanting and wanking their huge cocks, obviously participating in some carnal ritual. Nathan was also rock-hard, and he actually seemed to be enjoying this bizarre rite. He was obviously drugged. Or was he?

I screamed at the top of my lungs for them to stop and untie us. This just seemed to anger them. A wrinkled elder blurted out an order and two young, muscular bucks ran to me. They brutally lifted my feet, spread my legs wide, and stuck the snake up my ass. The pain was unbearable. I could feel the serpent squirming its way up my tight asshole.

All I could do was look on as the other savages relieved themselves on Nathan, bathing him with their piss. They then untied his legs and took turns butt-fucking him. One after another, after another, they dropped their loads inside him, and then went to dance around a campfire.

Finally, it was the turn of the two bucks who were holding me. They dropped me and ran to Nathan, fighting to see who would go first. One of them suddenly pulled out a knife and slashed the other one's throat. He then took his prize, fucking Nathan for several minutes until toppling on top of him. He looked spent, yet he soon joined the others around the fire.

I looked back and could barely see the snake anymore, for it had slithered its slimy self halfway up my ass. I was a curious sight indeed. It appeared as if I had a tail like some grotesque Centaur, the half-horse creatures from Greek Mythology. I tugged on the rope furiously until I was able to untie my hands from the pole. I then grabbed the snake and began to pull on it until I felt its fangs biting down on my prostate. It was clear to me; if I tried to pull it out, it would poison me. Aye, there was the rub.

But I would have to deal with the snake later. Freeing the kid was far more important. I ran to Nathan and began to untie him.

"It's okay, son," I said. "Don't worry; I'll get us out of this."

Nathan looked me in the face then. Only it wasn't Nathan anymore. He had the cold-blooded eyes of a reptile; and when he opened his mouth, his serpent-like tongue lashed out at me, grabbing me by the neck and choking me....

"Mr. O'Brien!" It was Nathan's voice. "Excuse me, Mr. O'Brien. You okay, man?"

My eyes snapped open and the sunlight flooded them with rays of reality. I was on the deck of my boat in the Miami Marina. I lay flat on my back, my legs in the air, with a twelve-inch dildo up my ass.

Shit! I had fallen asleep. And standing over me, with a quizzical look on his young face, was Nathan Landis.

"You are Mr. O'Brien aren't you?" he asked. "You're supposed to take me to the set."

"Yeah, I'm Jack O'Brien," I replied, blushing. "And I'm very embarrassed."

"Don't be," he said, kneeling next to me. "I start every morning the same way. Only my dildo is not as big as yours!"

I was utterly speechless. I just lay there dumbfounded.

"Take your time," Nathan added. "I don't have to be on set for hours. Maybe you can show me some of the more exotic sights. If you know what I mean?"

I gazed up and smiled blissfully at my dream boy. I guess dreams come true after all.

THE BOY TRAP

"Well, there's a devil in the angel,
And I'm in trouble again.
Well, there's a devil in the angel,
And I'm in need of a prayer."
—Bad 4 Good

This story takes place in the 70's. I had just turned eighteen. I was a junkie. I was confused. I was out of fucking control. I warn you, it's not for the faint of heart.

I guess I always knew I was a little different from other boys, as long as I could remember. And it confused the hell out of me, too. I mean, imagine an eleven-year-old boy watching "Flipper" on TV and popping a boner at the sight of Luke Halpin—Flipper's cute, little blond friend—in those wet, tight cut-offs.

Yes, I was a fickle youth. In fact, at eighteen I was still pretty fickle. But I had graduated from Luke Halpin to...Shaun Cassidy. Wow, what a babe! I collected every magazine that had his picture on the cover, so my closet was filled with stacks of "Tiger Beat" and "Teen Beat." They were all missing the centerfold, of course. Why? Because they were plastered all over my bedroom wall. I think that's when my mother first started suspecting that her only son was queer. I mean, most boys adorn their bedroom walls with posters of football teams, sports cars, and even the U.S.S. Enterprise. Aside from Shaun's big brother David, my walls were covered with Donny, Jimmy, and the rest of the Osmond Brothers.

Anyway, the moment of truth had finally come. After watching "Ode To Billy Joe" a dozen times—and fooling around with my best friend Vinnie Bonaducci—I'd finally come to the realization that I was a homosexual. And unlike Billie Joe McAllister, I wasn't jumping off no Tallahatchie bridge.

While I accepted the fact that I was different, I wasn't ready to admit that I was actually gay. My Uncle Bruce was gay, and I'd seen firsthand how cruel people could be. My father, for instance, called him a faggot every chance he got. They were brothers and they hadn't talked to each other for as long as I could remember.

Now I was going to walk into his den and tell him that his only son, his only child, his namesake, was a member of the same church as his black-sheep brother whom we never talked about. I was sure he was going to have a massive coronary.

I just hoped my dad wouldn't call me a faggot to my face. It wasn't like it was going to ruin our relationship or anything. We were strangers really, and we avoided each other every chance we got. I'd always sensed that he was disappointed in me. And that always pissed me off, too. I mean, I was a straight-A student; my room was anal-retentively neat; and in that day and age, I'd never been to the principal's office, let alone jail. Yet he was disappointed in me because I wasn't some dumbass sports fanatic like he was. He played college football and I think that kind of warps your mind a little. Also, the fact that I wanted to be an interior decorator didn't exactly help situations any. Wait till he found out I fooled around with his hunting buddy's son.

Well, I didn't mean to. It just happened. We were in his room after school, looking through his collection of girlie magazines and...well, one thing led to another...one hand led to another...one lip led to another...and pretty soon, Vinnie looked like The Lone Ranger riding Silver. It was quite dramatic really. Two days later, I was still glowing.

Unfortunately, the experience wasn't mutual. Vinnie's Catholic guilt hit him half a second after he shot the sheriff. He started saying we were both going straight to hell for being queens. He'd been shaving his palms twice a day for the last four years, but yet he was going to hell for doing it with me *once.* Then he had the nerve to accuse me of seducing him. He was the one who stuck his tongue in my mouth all the way to my tonsils. Anyway, he didn't know how he was going to bring himself to break this news to Father O'Brien during his next confession. After being one of the good Father's altar boys for a year, I assured him that Father O'Brien would more than understand...and probably even identify with him. That's when he threw me out.

I wasn't worried at all about my mother. You know what they say: the mother always knows. She'd probably cry. Then I'd cry. Then we'd both cry and embrace. It would be a Hallmark moment. I wished the rest of the world would be as open-minded as my mother. But I knew it wasn't. I knew it wouldn't be easy being gay in the 70's. Hell, it's never easy being different. People who didn't even know me would call me names and hate me, just because I happen to like men instead of women...no other reason. Macho guys, with one foot in the closet, would be repulsed by me because I remind them of a part of themselves they can't accept.

Girls who live in glass closets shouldn't toss pebbles.

Preachers would sentence me to eternal damnation just because some book of ancient mythology— the same book, by the way, that's caused most of the wars in this world—says that it's a sin to be what I am. But I couldn't live a lie. I couldn't be like one of those limp-wristed actors who went on Merv Griffin's show and sat there lying through their bonded teeth about all the women they'd had. I had to be honest with myself, and everyone else. That meant I had to tell my father.

I left my bedroom and began the slow walk downstairs to where my father sat, drinking a beer and watching baseball on TV. I couldn't help feeling like The Beaver about to tell Mr. Cleaver that he and Eddie Haskell were butt-buddies.

Well, *my* Ward Cleaver took it a lot worse than I thought he would. He began calling me every ugly, gay slur he could think of. Then he started beating me with his thick, black belt. When my poor mother tried to intervene, he began smacking her around too. At the end of it, he told me to get the fuck out of his house.

***

It was my third night on the streets when I first met Robin, the beautiful serpent whose apples were succulent, yet had many strings attached to their core. Hungry and desperate, I was dumpster-diving outside a grocery store. My little suburban world had collapsed and I just wanted to die.

Robin strutted out of the market in what looked like a Catholic school uniform. She was just barely carrying two giant bags of groceries, so when she looked up and caught me gaping at her, she called to me for assistance.

"Boy," she said, "could you please help?"

But it was too late. She'd dropped one of the bags, its contents spilling all over the parking lot. As I helped her stuff all the food back into the bag, I couldn't help ogling her divine figure, her shapely breasts, the way her long blonde hair got in her pretty face when she bent down to pick up something. I had never before lusted for a girl, and for a brief moment, I was excited at the prospect; maybe I was straight after all, and could soon go back home.

"Boy, I'll pay you five dollars if you help me carry my bags home," she said, blowing a wisp of curl off her face to reveal beauteous eyes of hazel. They were seductive eyes that could have enticed me into doing almost anything.

I said yes so fast that it brought a smile to her young face. Five bucks would mean a hardy dinner and breakfast at Mickey D's!

We walked four blocks down Biscayne Boulevard to her house. The bags were really heavy, and I was too hungry and sun struck to try to make small talk. She, on the other hand, was very inquisitive and somehow managed to get my life story out of me. Except for the part about my sexual orientation, of course.

I was a bit suspicious when we stopped in front of an old warehouse and she told me that was where she lived. However, I was too fatigued to question anything. She opened the warehouse door and we stepped into a disheveled office of sorts. The lights were dim, yet I could see the walls were plastered with photographs of naked young men sporting erections.

"What is this place?" I asked her, rather bemused.

"We make porno here," Robin said bluntly.

"Starring cute boys like you," said a hoarse, deep voice from behind me. "Good job, Robin."

I turned around to find a fat man who resembled Jerry Garcia from the Grateful Dead. He was dressed all in leather and was pointing a gun at me. Quite overwhelmed, I dropped the grocery bags and came dangerously close to passing out. A hand then reached into my back pocket and removed my wallet. It was Robin.

"I don't have any money," I blurted out, as tears filled my green eyes.

Robin found my drivers license. "His name is Tommy Syms and he's eighteen," she said, handing the license to the man.

"A bit skinny, but he'll do," he grunted. He then kicked a door open and pushed me into the next room.

As I got back on my feet, I realized I was in some cheap, makeshift movie studio. A Super-8 camera and a 35-millimeter still camera—not to mention half a dozen bright lights—were pointed at a king-sized, four-poster bed in the center of the warehouse. Old flats were erected around the bed to form what appeared to be a bedroom. Stranger still, the storage area to the side was chockfull of whips, rope, and ominous torture devices right out of a dungeon.

"Strip, twinky!" the man yelled at me.

I was visibly shaking, tears now running down my face. I looked to Robin for help. Surely, someone so beautiful couldn't be this evil.

"I have a surprise for you, boy," she said with an impish smile. She then turned her back to me and began to undress. Her smooth, androgynous figure looked even more appetizing buck-naked. She threw two flesh colored objects over her shoulder and they landed by my feet. They looked like latex tits. Then she turned around and I saw her (his!) cock.

A needle pricked my arm and a burst of euphoria consumed me. Then the room began to spin. I saw the fat man injecting me with a syringe before my innocent, boyhood world faded to black.

I awoke on the bed with the bright lights in my face. I was naked and ashamed. Feeling warmth on my genitals, I looked down to find Robin with my entire cock in his small, delicate mouth.

There was a pretty, fair-haired boy next to him who looked about my age. He too was naked and was busy licking my balls. I tried to move my hands, only to realize they were bound behind my back. I tried to move my legs, but my ankles were likewise tied. I made a futile attempt to scream, until it became apparently clear to me that my mouth was gagged with what appeared to be an old, smelly jockstrap.

The fat man hovered around us with a camera in one hand and his tremendous cock in the other. He ordered the boy, whose name was Shayne, to mount me. I didn't know what he meant until both Shayne and Robin spat on my cock and Shayne squatted over it, slowly lowering himself until my erection had disappeared up his petite ass. The boy did this flowingly as if he'd done it a million times before. He then began to move up and down on my cock, riding me while he furiously masturbated.

My body spasmed as I shot my load into the depths of the Shayne's ass. I felt the warmth when my seed trickled down his creamy buttocks onto my scrotum. Shayne began to quiver himself, obviously experiencing his own orgasm. His hot cum squirted everywhere, including all over Robin's face. He then fell on the bed beside me and pulled his butt cheeks apart. My jism was still oozing from his crack, so the fat man zoomed in on it with the camera and ordered Robin, who was more than willing, to lap it up with his tongue.

But that was not the climax of our little flick. No, the fat man had more in store for his new star. He called out the name "Secretariat." In the distance, an enormous black man, wearing only a leather mask, emerged from the darkness. His gargantuan cock led the way. A cock that was as long and fat as my forearm. I felt hands on my body then, rolling me over on my stomach. That's when I was struck by a scary revelation. I was about to be violated! And while Vinnie's modest cock felt great up my butt, this monster was going to tear me apart.

I think Robin saw the fear in my eyes, because he mercifully asked the fat man, whom he called Dale, to inject me with heroin once more. Dale produced the syringe from a nearby table and decided to shoot us all up.

Within seconds, that euphoric warmth again rippled through my young body. It was the answer to all my problems. For the first time in a long while I was happy. I had achieved a perfect state of nirvana and I never wanted to come down. I was an insatiable, sexual creature who yearned to have that big, black cock deep inside me to quench the fire that burned in my loins. I welcomed the pain, I welcomed the blood, I welcomed the degradation. I was living for that moment in time and it felt fucking great!

Secretariat plunged his horse cock into me with one hard thrust. And before I lost consciousness, for one brief shining moment, I thought I saw the face of God…And he was a black man.

***

"Wake up, twinky!" barked a man's voice.

Before I could open my eyes, I could feel my body was underwater. I was quite disoriented. My head was throbbing with pain and my ass felt like a colony of fire ants had invaded it.

Slowly, I remembered the motor skills that worked my eyelids. The part of me that hoped it had all just been a bad dream was greatly disappointed when my eyes focused on Dale. He was sitting on the edge of the bathtub, shaking me. I was *in* the bathtub submerged in bubbles.

"What the fuck...?!" I managed to get out.

"Calm down, twinky," he said. "It's all over...for now." He then shocked me by throwing a fifty-dollar bill into the tub. "That's your fee. And there's a lot more where that came from."

"What do you want from me?" I inquired, while snatching the bill and clutching it tightly in my right hand.

"Your soul," he quipped. "And you're going to hand it to me on a silver platter."

I began to get up.

"Sit down, motherfucker!" he snarled, and then pushed me down with all his might. "Let's get something straight, twinky! From now on, you work for me! And you will do everything I tell you to do! You will appear in my movies; you will let me and my friends fuck you; and you will wipe the shit from my ass with your tongue if I tell you to do it. And if you don't, I'll blackmail your ass. I went through your wallet, Tommy Syms. I know where your parents live; 146 Southwest 9th Avenue. I know where you go to school; Miami High. If you betray me, I'll mail your family and friends pictures of you being butt-fucked by a big, bad nigger. Not to mention all the stuff we made you do after you passed out. They're all gonna know that you're a queer, cocksucking faggot!"

One thing I've always had is a bad temper. He was pissing me off and I grew weary of the whole charade. It was time I took control.

"Are you finished?" I asked flippantly. "Because if you are finished with your idle threats, I think you'll be interested in what I have to say."

Dale was taken aback; he carefully eyeballed me for a moment, either studying me or trying to intimidate me. An amused look then took over his plump face. "Is that so?" said he.

"I'm sure those threats are very effective with all the scared young guys you bring here and exploit," I said, now sounding exceedingly cocky for a boy in my dire predicament. "But now that

I have my wits about me, I'm afraid I'm a little too smart to fall for that bullshit. First of all, it's obvious that the beautiful Robin and her—or should I say *his*—helpless grocery store scam is the bait you use to lure your victims here. Then you rape them and blackmail them to work for you. Second, let's say you were stupid enough to send those incriminating photos to my family and friends. I don't give a shit. You see, I have no use for those people anymore. I'm eighteen now; they're out of my life and, frankly, I don't care what the fuck they think of me. You can tell them I'm a transvestite necrophiliac if you want. But we all know that you're not going to tell or mail anyone anything. Because, third, you're guilty of the abduction and rape of a youth under twenty-one. The other boys and I may be eighteen or nineteen, but the legal age in this state to do porn is twenty-one. And I think making gay porn is even outlawed in Florida. The authorities would find you and throw your fat ass in jail so fast that it'll make your head spin. Especially if the victim, namely me, is ready and willing to testify against you."

Of course, I was bullshitting. I had pulled the entire thing out of my ass. I didn't know what the laws were. Lucky for me, Dale was more ignorant about Florida statutes than I.

The fat man studied my face once more. For a moment, he looked like he might grab my neck and drown me. "You think you got it all figured out, huh, hotshot?"

"I know I do," I assured him, not backing down. "And if the money's right, I know I can be an asset to your operation."

Dale was genuinely intrigued by now, if not blown away. "Go on," he said.

"You see, I'm not one of those straight boys you have to force to suck cock, I'm queer and I really enjoyed last night. I especially enjoyed the heroin. So you be good to me and I'll be good to you."

Dale stared at me coldly for what seemed an eternity. Then, between guffaws, he said, "Twinky, you're a fucking trip! And I'll tell you something, I feel safer having you as a friend than as an enemy."

"Does that mean we have a deal?"

Dale stood and aimed his cock at the toilet, releasing a powerful jet-stream of piss. "Only if you accept my terms," he said, turning his cock on my face without breaking the urine flux. "All my slave boys have to take my golden showers." By then, he had drenched my bemused face. "I hereby christen you...Twinky, prince of queer porn!" said Dale, the Sleaze-Baptist, with pride. He then jumped into the piss-filled tub with me and kissed me on the mouth. Thus began an exceedingly dysfunctional family.

***

Within weeks, I had *earned* the name, Twinky, prince of queer porn, by becoming Dale's right-hand man. It wasn't long before I was luring more sheep into the slaughterhouse than Robin—and with a much different approach. I would find guys, just over eighteen, on the streets and at bus stations—who were just as hungry and desperate as I had been. Then I would befriend them, gaining their precious trust. After that, it was easy. I'd just fill their puerile heads with sweet stories of easy money and free drugs. Once they were in the fold, it was up to Dale to drug and blackmail them.

I wanted to feel guilty for my actions, yet I was so strung out on smack all the time that my mind wouldn't entertain that emotion. Besides, in a way I felt that I was helping these unfortunates: I was putting money in their pockets so they wouldn't starve or have to live on the cruel streets. At least they weren't out stealing or hustling on the boulevard. And aside from the initial shock and pain, nobody was really getting hurt, were they? At the time, I didn't know that I was an expert at rationalizing.

I was making a small fortune too, with lots of cash in my pocket. And even though I was self-destructive and out of control, I must confess that I was having the time of my life. The sex was great! The drugs were awesome! The power was intoxicating! My sexual freedom was liberating! It seemed like I had it made in the shade.

Then I met Gabriel, and the world as I knew it got a lot more complicated—and *dangerous*.

I fell in love with Gabriel the moment I saw him emerge from the Greyhound bus. It was dusk and the setting sun's rays hit him like a spotlight, so there was this surreal radiance about him. An angel had somehow stepped off a Caravaggio painting and onto the Miami bus station. His divine wings had been clipped, but there was no doubt about it, this boy had descended from the heavens. Perhaps to save me. But could anyone?

I stood transfixed, watching him, studying him, devouring his young and slender form with my ravenous eyes. I had never before witnessed such natural splendor and I was overwhelmed. All my life I had been blind and this creature was the first glorious vision that my eyes beheld. That is the only way I could describe the emotions that deluged my mind at that moment.

The kid was a living, breathing paradox. He looked ragged, but seductively alluring nonetheless. Long chestnut hair fell over his callow face in an unruly yet enticing way. He seemed innocent, yet he was a very sexual animal, just oozing sensuality. His body was scrawny, but he moved with a feline, almost elegant, poise. Yes, a paradox. He was clad in blue denim: an old jacket and worn-out jeans. A faded skull on his t-shirt was the perfect contrast to his delicate face: the high cheekbones, the pouty lips, the flawless olive skin.

My lithe, young angel stopped to look around as he adjusted the timeworn knapsack strapped to his back. He seemed so lost and scared, unsure of his next move. It was sad how timid and alone this poor boy appeared. Every fiber of my being wanted to take his fragile body in my arms and protect him from the hawks that were always circling. But wasn't I a treacherous predator myself, a wolf in sheep's clothing, sent to infiltrate the unsuspecting flock and corrupt the virginal? Who was going to protect this boy from *me*?

He looked in my direction. With a quick jerk of his head, he flipped the hair off his face like a flirtatious girl and smiled at me. Our eyes met for the first time, kissing and caressing like old lovers. I could now see the lovely windows to his soul; they were baby blue.

Surely, bringing this prize to Dale would mean a big feather in my cap, not to mention a handsome finder's fee. But I just couldn't bring myself to do it. We would steal his innocence, then eat him up and spit him out. No, this boy deserved better. This boy deserved *much* better!

He began to walk towards me and I panicked. I couldn't give in to temptation! I had to be strong! I was determined that I wasn't going to ruin this boy's life. So I ran away from him before I changed my mind. I ran as fast as I could and never looked back.

I spent a few hours in the arcade, desperately trying to forget the boy in the bus station. His beauteous face, however, was forever imprinted in my mind. We were filming a movie at nine o'clock, so I went back home to the warehouse.

As I walked in the office, I noticed that they were already filming in the next room. Robin sauntered out to greet me, wearing only a thick dog collar and holding a bullwhip.

"Hey, twinky," he said. "How was the hunt?"

"I had a shitty day."

"I had an awesome day!" he bragged. "Wait till you see what I brought in. Dale almost came in his pants when he saw this one! God, he just turned eighteen and looks like a fuckin' altar boy!"

I was usually very competitive with Robin; however, all I could think about was shooting up.

"It was weird that we didn't run into each other today," Robin continued. "It was slim pickings out on the streets so I had to go to the bus station."

I felt sick to my stomach. I didn't even have to see him. I knew that the gods had played a cruel trick on me. After taking a deep breath, I walked on the set. Tears filled my eyes when I looked on the bed and saw my angel being sodomized by my fellow players. He was on his back, bound and gagged by Secretariat's stout cock, as the black man was fucking his virgin mouth.

"Come on, twinky, join the fun," said a jovial Dale from behind the camera. "Ain't he pretty?"

I forced myself to look into the boy's terrified face. His eyes turned to daggers as he stared at me with loathing. All I could do was mouth the words, "I'm sorry." I was about to cry for my broken heart, when Robin came to the rescue. He gave me the syringe and I was soon at peace.

The boy was now on his stomach. Shayne and his identical twin Dwayne were busy munching on his tiny pink hole while Secretariat lubricated his hard eleven inches with spittle, drooling in anticipation. The black stallion tried to shove just the head into the boy's crack at first, but it was simply too fat. It was like a boa constrictor trying to force its way into a wormhole. He looked to Dale for guidance.

"I don't care if it don't fit!" Dale barked. "Just pop his fucking cherry!"

Secretariat rammed his whopping shaft into him hard! I turned my head away when I noticed the cherry red blood streaming down the boy's milky white buttocks. That's when I saw Robin bringing in the Doberman.

I was overtaken by nausea and made a run for the toilet. As I knelt over the porcelain bowl emptying my guts, I knew that I couldn't take anymore. And I prayed to God for the strength to leave. Sadly, God didn't know who the hell I was anymore. Neither did I.

Morning came and I listened outside the bathroom door as Dale blackmailed my angel. The boy was frightened; and he was sobbing. He begged Dale not to send those nasty photos to his family and friends in Rome, Wisconsin. Dale assured him that if he played his cards right, no harm would come to him.

"Just don't fuck with me!" he snapped at the boy as he stormed out of the bathroom, walking right into my naked body. "What the fuck are you doing, twinky? Eavesdropping?"

"I need to take a bath," I said quickly.

Dale shoved his index finger up my ass, then brought it to his mouth and sucked it. "You're right, you do need a bath." Having amused himself, he let out a hearty laugh and walked away.

I stepped into the bathroom, locking the door behind me. The boy was crying in a tub of bubbles.

"Are you okay?" I asked.

He looked up at me with an accusatory stare. If looks could kill, I would have been fatally castrated at that moment.

"Were you their scout?" he inquired brusquely. "Is that why you ran off so fast when you saw me—to tell 'em that fresh meat had just gotten off the bus?!"

The boy couldn't have wounded me more if he *had* castrated me. "No, you've got it all wrong."

Shaking his head, he said, "Whatever, man."

I tried to think of something meaningful to say. Something eloquent and sensitive. However, all I could come up with was: "How do you feel?"

"How the fuck do you think I feel?!" he snapped. "How would *you* feel if you had just been fucked by a—?!" He began to weep again.

Overcome by an overwhelming urge to comfort the boy, I got into the bathtub with him, taking him in my arms like a baby. Instead of resisting, his body went limp against me. He gave himself to me completely as he cried on my shoulder.

"I'm sorry," I whispered. "I'm so sorry."

The boy looked into my eyes. "Why are you in here with me?" he asked coldly. "Is it your turn to fuck me now?"

"No. I would never force myself on you," I asserted.

"I bet you say that to all the boys...before you rape 'em."

"I mean it. I'm so sorry that this happened to you."

"Then why did you let it happen?!"

The boy hurt me deeply with those words. I felt like a worthless coward.

"What the hell could I have done about it?" I asked, trying to justify my humiliating cravenness.

"A lot more than you did, I'm sure."

"I was high...I was sick..."

"Spare me, man."

I felt like a loser in this boy's eyes. I had failed him miserably, and now I had to redeem myself somehow.

"I can help you now, though," I whispered, for the walls had ears. "Dale was bullshitting about the blackmail. You can leave and never come back and *nothing* will happen to you. I promise."

"Oh yeah," he said, skeptically. "If that's true, and you know it's true, then why are you here?"

"Because...I have no other place to go."

"Now who's bullshitting who? You're not like the others, you're not evil, you don't belong here."

"I need the smack, okay!" I blurted out, surprising myself with my enlightening admission.

"What's that?"

"You know, H. Heroin."

The boy experienced a revelation then. "That explains everything. You're a junkie. And I thought those were just mosquito bites all over your arms."

"Now do you see why I can't leave?" I confessed; the addict making more excuses.

"Back in Wisconsin, I was kind of a junkie too. I was hooked on three meals a day, a big house with central air, and all the toys I could play with. And even though I was dependent on my old man—the same way you're dependent on that Dale guy—I had to be strong enough to leave it all behind when I turned eighteen. And you have to be strong enough to do the same thing."

"Damn, you're smart for your age," I said, taken aback by his precocious insight.

He nodded. "In school they called me 'gifted' and separated me from the normal kids like a freak. They even put me in a different school full of freaks. To make things even worse, I was queer too. That's how everyone in town treated me, as the queer freak."

"Is that why you left home?"

"No," said the boy. He stood to show me his back. As the lather dissolved, I could see the black and blue marks beneath. "This is why," he said somberly, then fell into my arms once more.

"You're so beautiful," I said. "How could anyone do that to you?"

He then changed the subject, right out of the blue.

"Are you gay?"

"What makes you think that?"

"Oh, the way you looked at me at the bus station; the way you're looking at me now; your dick pressing into my stomach."

"I'm sorry."

"It's okay," he said, smiling for the first time. He then took hold of my hand and placed it on his budding erection. "I feel the same way."

I kissed him then—softly, delicately, lovingly—and he kissed me back, his wary tongue gingerly exploring my mouth.

"By the way, what's your name?" I asked him between kisses.

"Gabriel," he said.

"The Angel Gabriel," I muttered, laughing at the irony.

"What's yours?"

"Tommy."

"Oh, Tommy, it feels so good in your arms. I wish you could hold me forever."

"And I'll never let anyone hurt you again, my Gabriel."

He kissed me and I kissed him back, deeply, with as much passion as I could muster. Everything about him was intoxicating: the taste of him, the smell of him, the touch of his fervid, silky skin. My senses were overcome by manic exhilaration. I was *high* on him! And it felt more intense than any junk I could ever shoot up! Maybe I could be saved after all.

***

Through the hazy mist I could see a comely boy walking through a field, when he came upon a herd of sheep. A cuddly lamb soon caught his eye and he dropped to his knees to pet the creature. He caressed the lamb gently and methodically at first. But suddenly he pulled out a knife and cut its tender throat. I screamed when I saw the boy's face. It was my face! And the decapitated lamb wasn't a sheep after all. It was a nude boy with wings. His head laid next to his dead body, glaring at me with accusatory eyes. I screamed again when I realized...it was Gabriel! He lugubriously whispered the words: "Yet each man kills the thing he loves."

A deafening blast of thunder rattled the bed. I woke up in a cold sweat. A tidal wave of relieve struck and enveloped me when I looked over to find Gabriel sleeping in my arms. He was alive! I kissed his forehead and began to weep.

With the warehouse all to ourselves, we had apparently slept the day away. The other boys were at the arcade and it was Friday. Every Friday, Dale flew up to New Orleans for the day to deliver a week's worth of gay porn to his superiors. I gazed over at the clock and was suddenly filled with dread. Four o'clock! Dale would soon be home! I had to get Gabriel out of there before he returned! How could we have been so careless to allow ourselves to fall asleep?

Carelessness had nothing to do with it, said a voice from deep within me. *You need your fix and you're too much of a pathetic, cowardly wretch to split before daddy gets home with the goodies!*

Lightning struck outside with a blinding furor as the door suddenly swung open. A towering figure loomed from the darkness and approached the bed.

"Rise and shine!" he roared. "Daddy's home!" Dale grabbed my head and violated my mouth with his slimy tongue.

With Gabriel still soundly sleeping, Dale had me follow him to the office. Once there, he peeled off his wet clothes and set them to dry by the air vent.

"It's pouring outside!" he grumbled, then sat behind his desk buck naked, his fat hanging everywhere.

"How was your trip?" I inquired, pretending to care.

"Very productive," he said, with a maniacal smile. "They're very pleased with my work. That's why they're trusting me to organize their new venture. The next step. It seems the market is gettin' saturated with stuff from Europe. There's no money in it anymore. So we're gonna start makin' snuff films."

"What are snuff films?"

"Same old shit, except for one thing: during the climax, the model dies in a violent, bloody massacre."

"Like a horror movie."

"Yeah, I guess you could call it that," said Dale. He stood and commenced opening the safe over his desk.

"Cool. My favorite movie last year was 'Halloween.' They showed the making of it on TV and I learned how to make fake blood out of..."

66! Bingo!

He had been careless yet again and I finally had the last number to the combination.

"No, you don't understand," he said, taking a small bag of heroin out of the safe. "We use real blood. We use a real knife. We really kill the model."

A chill ran down my spine; the son-of-a-bitch was serious! All I could do was just sit there and stare at him with a benumbed face.

"Of course, we're going to need some new blood," he continued, unfazed. "I've grown quite close to you boys and I wouldn't dream of slaughtering you. But that new boy sleeping in there is perfect. So innocent, so pretty, just eighteen. He's going to be our first star. And you're the lucky bastard who's gonna get to slash his pretty little throat."

Yet each man kills the thing he loves.

I jumped to my feet. "Over my dead body!" I screamed.

"Oh, that can be arranged, twinky. But it won't come to that. You'll do it all right." He waved the heroin in my face. "And this is the only motivation you'll need." He glanced at his watch. "It's getting to be about that time again, ain't it? Time for your fix, junkie."

"You're fucking insane!" I cried. "I wouldn't kill Gabriel for all the junk in the world!" I picked up the phone. "I'm calling the cops!"

That's when he took his gun out of the safe. "Big mistake, twinky," he said ominously, pointing the .44 at my head. "You know, I'm very disappointed in you. You're my favorite, my protégé, my apprentice. I thought you had more backbone in you."

I dropped the phone when I heard him cock the pistol. Satan had me by the balls.

It was to be a closed set. Dale left a note on the door for the other boys. It read, "Away for the weekend. No trespassing!" But I doubted if anyone would even stop by. There was a tropical storm warning for Miami/Fort Lauderdale.

I wanted to make it as easy on Gabriel as possible, so I pleaded with Dale not to tell him about his unfortunate fate. Dale agreed. Not out of the goodness of his heart, he just wanted to see the surprised look on the boy's face when he felt the knife at his throat. We told him, instead, that this was the last film either of us ever had to do for Dale. Afterwards, we would be released from our commitment and sent on our way with a hundred bucks each. Gabriel resisted at first, but he finally gave in when he saw that I was in favor of it. The poor unsuspecting fool actually trusted me.

With the bright lights pointed at us and Dale at the camera, we began rolling. The first part of the film was routine enough. Gabriel and I sucked each other off, and then he ate out my ass. Dale wanted us to kiss, but I just could't bring myself to kiss the poor soul that I was about to betray. That's when Gabriel first started to suspect that something was terribly wrong.

Dale ordered the boy to roll over, then told me to mount him from behind. I was angry at myself for having an erection. And I was frightened. Some part of me was getting off on this whole depraved scene. Maybe I was a lot more like Dale than I wanted to admit to myself.

Gabriel took my cock up his ass with no trouble at all, Secretariat had seen to that the night before. After a good five minutes of steady humping, Dale ordered the boy to roll on his back for the "money shot."

I sat on Gabriel's chest, with a leg on each side of his head, my hard cock throbbing just inches away from his pink lips. He looked up at me with his big, sad eyes and that's when I realized what I had to do. After I took the boy's life, I was going to slash my wrists and take my own.

Dale directed me to give his face a good fucking, so I did just that. Moments later, I experienced what I knew would be my last orgasm on this earth, shooting a hefty load all over Gabriel's face. Dale then stood over us with the camera and handed me the knife.

"It's time, twinky," he said in a foreboding tone.

The boy was dumbfounded. I could feel his small frame shaking beneath me.

Dale removed a syringe from the knapsack by his feet. "Come on, junkie," he said. "The sooner you do it, the sooner you get this."

I held the knife tightly in my shaking hand and brought it to Gabriel's throat.

"That's a good junkie," said Dale.

The room began to spin then. I was on some kind of macabre carousel. The only thing my eyes could focus upon was the needle oozing junk.

"Do it, junkie, do it!" Dale ordered.

My brain bade my hand to start carving. I could feel the blade pressing into the boy's neck.

That's when I heard him say, saying, "I love you, Tommy."

"No!" I wailed. "No!" I dropped the knife on the bed next to Gabriel's hand.

Dale tossed the syringe aside to remove his gun from the holster he wore around his naked waist. He put the barrel to my forehead with one hand and pointed the camera at it with the other.

"Pick up the knife and snuff him out, motherfucker!"

"No! You're gonna have to shoot me, you vile piece of shit!"

"With pleasure," he said dropping the camera, cocking the gun. "Good bye, twinky, ex-prince of queer porn."

I closed my eyes, bracing for severe pain, followed by forever darkness. Then I heard the loud bang! But I felt no pain. I opened my eyes to find Dale convulsing with the entire length of the knife plunged into his gut and blood gushing everywhere. I seized the moment to knock the gun out of his hand. It went off when it hit the floor and I realized then that the previous bang had merely been thunder.

Blood began to pour from Dale's mouth just as he toppled over us, driving the knife deeper into his bowels. Gabriel and I quickly got out from under Dale's bloody body on the bed. I took Gabriel in my arms and kissed him lovingly on the lips.

"I don't know what came over me," the boy said, weeping. "I couldn't let him kill you. I just picked up the knife and shoved it into him as hard as I could."

"It's all right, my love," I assured him. "You did good. Now let's get outta here."

I had Gabriel take the incriminating film from the camera, just in case we needed it in the future. Meanwhile, I opened the safe and was pleasantly surprised. The bastard had over fifty thousand dollars in hundred dollar bills neatly stacked inside. I shoved all the cash into my bag, along with all my personal belongings, and told Gabriel to do the same.

After washing Dale's putrid blood from our bodies, we got dressed, got our bags together, and locked the warehouse door behind us. Yes, it was *all* behind us.

I took my angel's hand in mine and we ran out into the pouring rain.

"Where to?" he asked.

Laughing joyously, I answered, "Everywhere, my love! Everywhere!"

JULIAN:
A CREATURE OF THE NIGHT

"I am Julian," whispered the creature with the angelic face to Martin, who was stunned, yet entranced by such ethereal beauty. And once again Julian engulfed Martin's whole penis in his tender mouth.

He was born Julian Cardinot in St. Petersburg, Missouri in the year of our Lord 1835. Because he was made into a creature of the night as a youth, he still retained the appearance of a lad in his late teens, although he was well over a hundred and forty years old.

He had slept—a prisoner in his own sarcophagus—for a hundred and twenty-nine of those years, until he finally awakened in the year 1976. There he walked the night streets, hunting for prey to feed upon—to satisfy his unquenchable thirst.

After posing as a prostitute to lure a handsome, male victim, he became curious about sex; what it would actually feel like. He was, after all, the world's oldest virgin. In his time, sexual intercourse with another male was considered a lewd, unconscionable act. But in the 1970's, though still controversial, it was quite acceptable to those enlightened mortals who cruised the boulevards late at night searching for pretty, young boys like himself. So he decided to give in to his curiosity. Instead of feeding on the attractive older man who had picked him up in the big automobile—as he had originally planned to do—Julian allowed the lusty stranger to do with him what he pleased.

He took Julian down a dirt road to a clearing by the Mississippi River. There, the man pulled down his pants and forced Julian's head down to his crotch. His huge penis was standing erect, the way Julian would awaken to find his own penis so many mornings—oh so long ago, before mornings became his enemy. He was enthralled by it, though he didn't know why. All he could do was stare at this appetizing sight and wonder what his customer wanted him to do with it.

"Hey, punk, if you wanna get paid, you better suck my cock!" the man ordered.

At first, Julian thought his request was absurd, but he decided to do it nonetheless. Gently he wrapped his soft lips around it, placing only the head in his virgin mouth.

It tastes pleasant enough, he thought.

But then, with one hard downward thrust, the man shoved the entire thing in his mouth.

In utter shock, Julian began to gag on it. He was about to break free from the bastard with his immortal strength, when it happened. It filled his hungry mouth with a sudden gush, sending him into complete ecstasy while he ejaculated in his trousers.

That is when Julian discovered that he had another hunger just as strong, just as passionate, as his thirst for blood: his hunger for men's semen. Though it could not sustain him by animating his immortal body as did the red life-force, he soon began to crave it just as much. So he became a male prostitute permanently, for it satisfied all of his immediate needs.

He was still lost, lonely and confused though. Julian was convinced that a mortal man—though good for a night of wild, animal passion—could not provide the companionship he so desperately needed. So he traveled south, looking for more of his kind. He missed so his nineteenth century world, and longed to be back where it all began.

***

The son of a blacksmith, the lad had lived his short mortal existence as a stable boy at the plantation where his father was employed. He worked from sunset to sundown, keeping mostly to himself—and to the horses he tended to and loved. They were his only friends really. And to Julian there was nothing greater than riding his beloved stallion, Comet, bareback and bare-assed through the dark countryside. It was grand! That intoxicating feeling of freedom; the icy wind making his long, black hair billow in the moonlight; and the feeling of his naked body pressing against the sweaty, warm blooded stud he mounted and rode like the wind. Looking back, he marveled at how he had always been a night creature really, because he lived for those midnight gallops. Then Julian's entire world changed when Jean-Pierre came into his life.

He was supposed to be the son of the plantation owner's distant cousin, visiting from France. Of course, none of them had ever seen a real Frenchman in person, so they just assumed they all looked as strange as Jean-Pierre. Not that he was homely. On the other hand, he was quite the handsome rogue: tall, muscle-bound, the chiseled face of a Michelangelo statue. Jean-Pierre just looked different. An elegant man in his early twenties—or so he appeared—his soft, beautiful skin was almost a luminescent white and his eyes were the brightest shade of green that Julian had ever seen. They appeared hypnotic almost.

The Frenchman became taken with the lad from the first time their eyes met. Julian too was taken with him, though he had never before experienced such feelings for another man—or woman, for that matter. His confusion frightened him, thus he avoided Jean-Pierre as much as he could. Which was exceedingly easy, for the mysterious visitor never seemed to be around in the daytime.

One night, Julian lay in a deep sleep, dreaming that Jean-Pierre and he were passionately kissing on the lips, their tongues dancing in each other's mouths. His long johns suddenly became damp and he awakened to find Jean-Pierre standing at the foot of his bed, naked; just staring at him while he jerked on his immense prick. Quite frightened by this unexpected, yet erotic sight, Julian quickly turned his head away but for a second. When he looked back, the Frenchman was gone as if he had been only an apparition. The following morning, Julian disregarded the entire thing as a very realistic dream.

The times he did run into Jean-Pierre after dusk, the lad noticed that the Frenchman looked at him as if in awe of an object of great beauty. The same way his mistress looked at the priceless paintings in the great halls of the plantation. All Julian could do was smile back at him, then go on his way; wondering why he felt warm all over.

He had never really thought much about his appearance in his eighteen years. Julian just assumed he was an average-looking, young man. Then after one of his encounters with the Frenchman, he disrobed in front of the full length mirror in his shack and carefully studied his reflection; searching to find what it was that Jean-Pierre found so exquisite. But his eyes were not the only ones feasting on his naked form. A feeling abruptly came over him that he was being watched. Hastily, he looked toward the window to find a radiant face gawking at him from the night. It was Jean-Pierre's. Again Julian was startled. He rapidly turned his head away from the sparkling eyes that licked his body with a hot tongue. As before, the Frenchman was gone when he looked back.

That night, Julian undressed in front of Comet as he did many nights. He was about to mount the animal, when Jean-Pierre appeared from the darkness. The lad was stunned, but more curious than afraid. In the blink of an eye, the swift stranger was standing in front of him, devouring him with his stare. He then reached over with his pale hand and began stroking Julian's hair. That awestruck look once more took over his face; but it was somehow different this time—melancholy.

"Oh, Julian," he spoke softly with his poetic accent. "You are the embodiment of divine beauty. A tender young god standing next to a devil. Such a lustrous mane of black curls; such innocent eyes sparking like hazel crystal; such clear, soft skin and delicate features—almost effeminate, but yet boyish; such sensuous, pouty lips; and such a callow, slender torso and firm, rounded buttocks." Tears were now rolling down his face. But they were not normal tears; they were red.

Julian was completely transfixed; his feet seemed rooted to the ground. He wanted to say something, yet nothing would come out of his mouth.

"So virginally pure you are, my Julian," he continued. "Would that I could only make time stand still to preserve such beauty. But alas, time stands still for no mortal and it shall too pierce your skin, mercilessly destroying a living, breathing work of art. What a shame. What a pity." He thought for a moment and then said, "However, it doesn't have to be like that, my young one. I cannot allow it to be like that! Within me I have the power to maintain you as you are for all of eternity. You shall be my progeny!"

The vampire opened his mouth wide, revealing sharp fangs. Before the lad could run, he was already drinking from the artery on his neck. Both their hearts began to beat as one, then the mortal world went dark for Julian.

And thus, the lad Julian Cardinot became the Julian the vampire. Jean-Pierre was his friend and his mentor; however, before he could become his lover, tragedy struck. Julian's father, a crazed religious fanatic, discovered their little secret.

At high noon one day, he found the cozy lair Jean-Pierre had made for them in the plantation house basement. He lifted the lid off Jean-Pierre's sarcophagus and burned him before he could awaken. Julian awoke to his horrid, doomed screams.

Desperately, he tried to push the lid off his own sarcophagus, only to find his father was wrapping chains around it. The old man kept repeating that Jean-Pierre and Julian were evil; that it was God's will for them to be destroyed. He didn't have the heart to burn his own son though. Instead, he buried him in the basement, as Julian pleaded with his father to release him. There he slumbered until the chains finally rusted away and he was able to dig his way out of the earth. But everything he had ever known and loved was gone.

***

"Swallow it, yeah swallow all of our cum, you cheap little whore!" demanded the hairy man with the large belly. Jean-Pierre's progeny lay on the floor in a tawdry Miami motel room, surrounded by ten, brawny naked sailors. The fleet had just come in and they were horny for a tender, young lad with an angelic face. So they had pooled their money together to buy him for a night of endless orgasms. They called it an orgy. Julian called it heaven.

If they only knew that their young angel was really an ancient demon; a fiendish, pretty wolf disguised as an innocent sheep, he thought, rather amused.

On his back, with his legs pulled open, the sailors used Julian as a group toy. One violated his tight ass with hard, steady thrusts. Two others sucked his plump balls while a third went down on his throbbing organ, giving him what they called, "head." Yet another licked the smooth envelope of flesh that covered his stomach, tickling his velvet torso with a flickering tongue. Two others gnawed at his perky nipples, not breaking the skin, but savoring the taste of immortal veal. The last three knelt over his face, shoving their pulsing, huge erections into his small, but accommodating, mouth. They came together, flooding his oral cavity with an endless spurt of that creamy, white daddy's milk that he had come to love so much.

The sailors had taken turns penetrating him all night long—and subjecting him to everything else they could possibly imagine. At one point, they inserted a peeled banana up his anus, leaving half sticking out. They then plopped scoops of Rocky Roads ice cream around it, added whipped cream on top, and topped it with a juicy cherry. At the count of three, the ravished sailor men commenced eating his love-hole like contestants devouring a sweet cherry pie at a pie-eating contest. The winner sucked up the banana half that was still lodged in his ass and swallowed it whole. They called this strange ritual an "Asshole Banana Split."
    When they were finally so exhausted that they couldn't take any more, they paid him his fee and fell fast asleep. Julian too was drained. Thirsting for his life-force, he fed on them as they slumbered. As always, never enough to kill them; just enough to satisfy his thirst. Jean-Pierre had told him that most vampires killed their prey when they fed. Julian, however, could never bring himself to kill something so lovely as a human male. Since he really didn't care for the taste of females, this was his only option. Of course, there was always the danger that the tiniest droplet of his life-force would enter their bodies, transforming them into the monster he had become. Julian didn't wish that damnation on anyone. But it was a risk he had to take.
    The young vampire existed in Miami for months like that, engaging in night after night of endless, meaningless sex. He desperately attempted to seek more of his kind by scanning the thoughts of all creatures he encountered, with his supernatural mind. Alas, all he found were mortals who were as miserable as he was. They feared their inevitable death, while he feared existing forever. How ironic...and how sad, he thought.
    Yes, Julian was fulfilled when it came to carnal pleasures. However, his loneliness was eating away at him like ants at a helpless insect. Many times he pondered pouring gasoline on his graceful body and striking a match to it. Then on the night Julian finally built up enough courage to do it—he met *him*.
    Julian never thought he could have such beauteous feelings for a mortal. But Martin—a striking older man with hair of ash and a truly benevolent soul—was quite unique. And in falling in love with him, he fell in love with "life" all over again.

***

After his beloved Andrew passed away, Martin was convinced that he was doomed to live the lonely life of a middle-aged, gay man: the superficial bar scene where anyone over fifty, no matter how distinguished or good-looking, was considered a troll; picking up hustlers on the boulevard, not so much for the sex, but just to hold someone; and frozen dinners for one, next to your only companions, the many pussycats you've adopted—settling for whatever unconditional love you can get. Though he was wealthy, healthy, and still quite dashing, Martin did not look forward to that bleak future. Then came that magical, midsummer night's dream...that turned out not to be a dream at all.

Martin was floating on a cloud, stark naked. He felt a familiar, warm sensation on his penis, bringing a smile to his face. Naturally he knew what it was and looked down expecting to see his precious Andrew's loving face. Instead, he saw a celestial vision. He was disappointed it was not his departed lover, of course. Nonetheless, being an aesthetic man, he was delighted to see such natural splendor.

Plato wrote that there is a moment when we catch a glimpse of the divine, reflected perhaps in the beauty of a face or figure. This is what he saw now. Such heavenly beauty possessed this creature that it brought tears to Martin's eyes. The warm feeling spread throughout his body then, filling him with a soothing sense of well being and happiness. Next came the sudden burst of pure euphoria that made him spasm and open his eyes.

Martin was no longer on the cloud, but in his cozy bed in the master bedroom of his modest estate. Yet the vision still remained. The moonlight spilled in on the creature, making the pale skin on his naked form seem even more luminescent. He was bent over the man's groin, holding his limp penis in his gentle hand, as semen trickled down his chin.

Was he still dreaming or was this creature for real? Martin was not sure. He only knew that he was in love, and he didn't want whatever it was to go away…ever.

"Who are you?" he managed to ask with a lump in his throat.

"I am the Julian the vampire," whispered the creature with the angelic face to the man, who was stunned, yet entranced by such ethereal beauty. And once again he engulfed Martin's whole penis in his tender mouth.

Martin naturally did not believe him, yet he was amused and intrigued by his outlandish answer. He then asked, "And why are you here, Julian the vampire?"

Julian removed the man's penis from his mouth to answer, even though it was rapidly growing again.

"As I walked by your home, I heard your thoughts," stated the young vampire. Tears of red were now leaking from his eyes. "They moved me as no mortal has ever moved me before. You are the companion I have been searching for, Martin Warner."

Martin was speechless. Tears also escaped his blue eyes. How did he know his name? And those red tears! If this was a dream, he hoped he would never awaken.

Julian climbed on top of Martin and kissed him full on the lips. Their two lonely tongues greeted each other, played and frolicked a little while, then made love like old friends.

Martin rolled Julian on his back, still kissing him hard. Leaving the lad's soft lips, he kissed his way down his fleecy body. He licked the young vampire's delicious milk, his smooth as marble armpits, his callow chest and stomach—and then rested at his erect cock.

Martin smiled at the sight of such an adorable penis. It wasn't big, but its almost perfect shape more than made up for it. He lovingly placed it in his mouth, tasting everything it had to offer.

The sweet scent that emanated from Julian's body was intoxicating. It made Martin's head spin in pure ecstasy. Sex had never felt so good, so right. Never! Not even with his Andrew.

Martin turned Julian over on his stomach, so's to feast upon his rounded ass. Pulling apart the supple cheeks, he commenced to eat the flaming hole that was just begging for a wet tongue to relieve its lusty heat. The young vampire groaned. Many a mortal had made a meal of his bum, but it was never like this. The man's tongue was a moist serpent, tempting its slimy way deep into the promised land.

The man then penetrated Julian, plunging his pulsating nine inches of manhood into what appeared a virgin ass. The immortal anal muscles were as tight as the day the creature was made, thus all his lovers had the privilege of popping his cherished cherry.

"Fuck my arse, Daddy!" the young vampire panted. "Fill me with your scolding, mortal juice!"

Martin lay over Julian, humping him like a wild dog in heat. The rhythm of their pelvic thrusts matched their racing hearts as the man shot his burning daddy's milk into the abyss of the lad's receptive love-hole.

Martin turned Julian over and began to go down on him, but Julian stopped him. "Before you swallow me, do you wish to remain with me for all of eternity?" the young vampire asked.

"Yes!" escaped from Martin's mouth before he could stop it. But that was exactly what he felt. For some reason, he loved this lovely creature and never wanted to be apart from him. "Yes, forever, my love."

Julian exposed his fangs to a benumbed Martin, who until then only half believed he was truly a vampire. Before he knew what hit him, the man was close to unconsciousness, as the young vampire drained him near death. "You must now drink back my life-force," said Julian lovingly, positioning his hard penis in front of Martin's mouth.

"But how?" Martin was able to utter, convinced he was about to die; murdered by this beauteous archangel he still loved and forgave.

A mischievous smile appeared on Julian's face. "My dear Martin, my tears are not all that is red."

With that, Julian placed his erection in Martin's mouth. He quickly ejaculated, Martin swallowing every last drop of it. As he began to feel stronger and better than ever, Martin knew exactly what his angel had meant.

Julian the vampire and his progeny Martin leapt from the bedroom's second story window into the night. They ran hand in hand, never to be lonely again, and looking forward to the many adventures that awaited them in centuries to come.

Another vampire appeared from the shadows then. Jean-Pierre looked upon his progeny, and the vampire he begot, with an overwhelming sense of sadness. He had searched for his beloved Julian for such a long time, only to find him in love with another immortal. He truly could not blame him though. After all, Julian did not know that when you burn a vampire, you must scatter its ashes, or they will regenerate and the creature will rise from them like the phoenix. It may take over a hundred and twenty years, but the vampire will return.

Crimson tears streamed down Jean-Pierre's face. He would never see his beloved Julian again.

EDDIE'S AUDITION

"I don't need a lot; Only what I got.
Plus a tube of greasepaint and a follow spot."
—Sondheim

Why aren't greenrooms ever really green? the boy thought, staring at the peach wallpaper. *Why does "five minutes, señor" always turn into fifteen minutes because the ham ahead of you just has to squeeze out two encores before finally leaving the stage?*

He looked around the room. The Spanish chatter sounded almost foreign to him, like chicken clucking. He had been away so long.

But these weren't normal chickens. No, they were the *crème de la crème* of show biz fowl. And he was right smack in the middle of the prestigious hen house.

But why?! He wasn't in their league. Did he deserve to be there—*again*? He really didn't know. He only knew he was sick to his stomach, and his hands were shaking so badly, he couldn't even hold a cup of water without spilling some all over his costume. He wanted out of there. Oh, he wanted out of there badly. He wanted to rip off the tight show clothes that bound him; change back into his comfortable sweatpants, T-shirt, and Reeboks; and get the hell out of there. *Run* the hell out of there, as a matter of fact, past his shiny stretch-limo, through the crowded streets of Mexico City, then to the sea. Where he would swim across the Gulf back home to Florida. The idea was very appealing. Hell, the idea was almost unbearable to resist.

Yet deep inside, he knew he couldn't do it. He had invested so much time and energy into this, his "big comeback," that now he just had to go through with it. After all, getting on that show hadn't been easy. In fact, it had been a big coup for his agent. This was the big break he'd been waiting for. His debut as a solo artist.

"Siempre En Domingo" was the premiere variety show of all Latin America. Though the new album was a modest success, his performance that night would make or break his solo career—and he knew it. He knew it all too well. He had to go out there and, not just be *good*, but blow them away. He had to prove to the world—and mostly to himself—that he wasn't a has-been ex-child-star from a "manufactured" teenybopper group. That he was a *real* singer with *real* talent. And that he didn't need his four little sidekicks to back him up.

But he *did* need them. He never needed them more in his life. Not so much their bodies out on the stage with him, as their moral support. Looking around at all the famous faces in that room, he never felt more alone, more inadequate. Sure they smiled back at him when their eyes met, yet they weren't real smiles. They were as fake as the people who donned them: envious, back-stabbing egomaniacs who wouldn't think twice about cutting your throat to advance their precious careers.

He couldn't remember how many times he'd met stars who seemed so nice on TV, but were really bastards and bitches in person. He had been a fan of so many of them—almost worshipping the ground they walked on, in some cases—only to be crushed upon meeting them. Behind all the smiles in that room, he knew there was an underlying feeling of scorn and competitiveness. They didn't wish him well. In all actuality, they hoped he would fail miserably so *they* would be the hit of the show. God forbid he stole that dear spotlight away from them. He needed sincere moral support at that moment, and those phony smiles just weren't doing it.

He longed for Carlito, Rico—even Chico. Most of all, he longed for his beloved Juanie. Sweet, benevolent Juanie. He would know the right things to say to calm his nerves. Best of all, Juanie would hold him. He would hold him that dread moment before stepping out on the stage—when your heart jumps to your throat, almost choking you. Oh, how he wished his Juanie were there.

One of the assistant stage managers again came in the room. "Cinco minutos, Señor," said the bald, little man wearing the headset to the boy. Tito Puente was in the middle of his second encore, and this time the stage manager really did mean "five minutes."

The boy stood, only to find his knees were made of rubber. The stench of caviar, champagne, and cheese that permeated the room suddenly kicked him in the stomach, making him almost vomit on Maria Conchita Alonso. Paul Rodriguez shook one of his clammy hands and told him to break a leg, while the voluptuous Xuxa patted him on the back with one hand as she pinched his ass with the other.

He followed the stage manager to the wings, all the time searching for the nearest exit, just in case he built up enough courage to make a run for it. Then, as he approached the enormous stage, a tidal wave of total recall struck and enveloped him, almost knocking him over with its awesome magnitude. It all came back to him then: the first time they did the show; all the concerts; the screaming fans stampeding the stage and ripping at his clothes; the horny groupies; the drugs; and, oh yes, the hot nasty sex. More than four years had passed—almost five—yet he suddenly remembered all of it as if it were yesterday. When he went from poor, Cuban refugee Eduardo José Pacheco to EDDIE, singing star of Los Muchachos. And it had all begun that fateful day he came across that newspaper ad. The ad that changed his humdrum life forever. It was in the Entertainment Section of "The Miami Herald," sandwiched between "Friday The 13th VII: The New Blood" and "Salsa: The Motion Picture." He could still see the ad in his head like it was only yesterday.

"Open Call. International Talent Search for boys 12 to 15 to join Latin pop sensation, Los Muchachos. No experience necessary, but some singing & dance training is preferred. Boys must be cute, speak Spanish, and look good in tight clothes. Be a teen idol and see the world! Auditions will be held at 11 a.m., Saturday, June 4th. Gusman Center, 175 East Flagler Street, Downtown Miami."

"That's tomorrow!" Eddie exclaimed, alarmed and excited at the same time. His big brown eyes were glued to the ad in front of him.

He was supposed to be looking through the Help Wanted Section, of course. That was the only reason his mother had seen fit to spend an entire quarter on the paper.

Money was very tight and every penny counted. That quarter could have easily bought a package of Campbell's Ramen Noodle Soup; they were four for a dollar at the neighborhood Sedanos'

Supermarket. It wasn't exactly nutritious, the poor-man's soup, but those thick noodles and that chicken-flavored broth could sure fill you up on nights when there was nothing else in the kitchen cupboard or in the refrigerator, except for a can of generic cat food. The worst part was, they didn't own a cat. The no-frills feline cuisine was there for an emergency. Luckily, they had never been that hungry, though many a time they had come close. Too close.

Eddie's mother did her best to provide for herself and her only son, her only living family. She broke her back every day, waitressing at Los Cubanitos Restaurant in Little Havana. But a waitress only earns so much...especially at a dump like Los Cubanitos. And her drinking didn't help things either.

She started hitting the bottle back in Cuba after Eddie's father was executed for attempting to organize a coup against the Castro regime. Eddie was only ten months old. Five years later, Maria Pacheco and her young son made it to America as part of the infamous Mariel Boat Lift: a flotilla of hundreds of private vessels that carried refugees from Mariel, Cuba to Key West in the spring of 1980. They were hungry, thirsty, and frightened; but they were *libre*—free. They had made it.

Now, eight years later, they were just barely making it. Eddie's mother was drinking more and more, and they had less and less every day. She went from one abusive boyfriend to another, searching for love and security, but ending up with heartache and unpaid long-distance phone bills instead. Some of the men were nice enough, yet most of them were violent freeloaders who drank more than his mother. She had a knack for picking losers, Eddie always thought. Except for his father, of course. Eddie idolized him, though he didn't remember him really. Yet he was proud to have the blood of a brave revolutionary running through his veins. Eddie could have been the son of Cuba's first democratic president that century. Instead, he was stigmatized as a dread Marielita: the popular Miamian word for Cuban trash.

He had to help his mother make ends meet, thus he had been looking for a summer job that Friday afternoon. But he could never pick up a newspaper without looking through the entertainment section first. He'd always dreamed of some day being in show business. In his fantasies—and there were a lot of them—it was his way out of the Cuban ghetto he and his mother were forced to live in. And why not? After all, show business *was* in his blood.

His father had been a somewhat famous stage actor in Cuba before he got involved with politics. That's how he'd met his mother; she was a dancer in a show he was starring in. That would explain why Eddie always had that basic, instinctual need to perform. He just loved being in front of a crowd, entertaining. And since his mother had taught him to sing and dance before he could walk almost, the boy was quite good. Though he only got a chance to show it off at school talent shows and on slow nights at Los Cubanitos when—accompanied by his mother on the guitar—he would make the patrons cry with old songs from the homeland. He and his mother would make out like bandits in tips on those nights. "No one tips better than an old, crying Cuban yearning for home," Maria used to say jokingly. When she joked and didn't have a hangover, that is.

"Los Muchachos," Eddie muttered, brushing the long strands of auburn hair out of his eyes. He remembered seeing them on all the Spanish variety shows his mother watched in between "novellas." He wasn't really a fan of their music. He preferred real dance music as opposed to the pop, bubblegum stuff that Los Muchachos did. Besides, he'd always thought they looked a bit tacky in their matching polyester costumes. However, for some odd reason, he could never take his eyes off the boys when he'd walk by the TV and they happened to be on. He even secretly wished he could afford to buy concert tickets when he found out they were performing that weekend at the Gusman Center. He quite honestly didn't know what it was about them that fascinated him so. Was it their music? Was it the synchronized choreography? Was it their cute, little...?

Whatever it was, he was embarrassed by it. After all, Los Muchachos' only fans where horny teenage girls—everybody knew that—*not* boys. It was sissy stuff. And he was no sissy. Not the son of a revolutionary!

What he *was*, was excited at the thought of actually being a Muchacho, being famous, being rich, performing in front of millions. The images racing through his mind were intoxicating, filling him with a strange, warm sensation that made his small body tingle and his pinga stand at attention. But ever since he started getting hair down there, the darn thing would stand at the drop of a hat. And, at the most inopportune of times. For instance, kneeling in the church confessional, at the sound of Father Garcia's husky voice; and in the school shower room after gym class. It was like it had a mind of its own. It was embarrassing.

Eddie wanted to run into the living room and show his mother the audition ad. She had just gotten home from work and would soon take her first drink of the day. This would lead to the nightly drunken stupors he had reluctantly learned to live with. The boy wanted to get his mother while she was still coherent. God knows he sure as hell avoided her when she was sauced. Yet, he certainly couldn't parade into the living room with his underpants a small, white tent.

He had two options: either think of something really gross to make the bulge subside, or do what he learned by spying on one of his mother's boyfriends five years back while she was at work. The latter somehow seemed a more pleasant option. It always did. Ever since he copied what his "Stepfather of the Month" was doing on the couch that morning he had the flu and was forced to stay home from school. He had just stood behind the man, imitating his every move, his every jerk. He couldn't however copy the man's spectacular finale—not for four more years that is. He'd never forget the first time it happened. It was quite a pleasant surprise, the new sensations, poor George Michael's face dripping wet on the poster over his bed, all of it. It's one of those things guys always remember. Like your first car.

Eddie put a chair up against his bedroom door. He then lay back in bed on his old "Return of the Jedi" bedspread—soiled from the many times before—and pulled down his Fruit of the Looms. It was up all right, at twelve o'clock on the dot. The boy spat into his left palm—he was a lefty—and closed his eyes, letting his wet hand wander down his tender body to the carnal playground.

Around him, the faces of his favorite stars looked down at him from the many posters on the walls—not passing judgment, but sharing in this sacred, boyhood ritual.

He would have normally thought of the dirty pictures in the "Hustler Magazine" he'd found in the back alley behind Los Cubanitos. His mother had unfortunately come across it while cleaning his room and—like any good Catholic mother—had thrown it away. But not before he'd memorized every single dirty photo in the magazine. This time, however, he didn't seem to need it. For reasons beyond his comprehension, just the mental pictures of him with Los Muchachos—singing and dancing and showering after a concert, soaping each other's—

Squirt!

Eddie was able to reach his mother before the first drink. She was so excited by the whole idea, that she didn't even take one swig of vodka—her poison of choice as Eddie thought of it—that entire night. Instead, she helped her son prepare an audition.

"I seen dos boys perform a million time," she told him in her broken English, which she now spoke as much as possible for the practice, "and dey got nothing on jew, baby." Her face then filled with pride. "Jew have real talent. Pacheco Family talent. It's in jour yenes!"

Maria and her son worked into the night, perfecting every last bit of his audition routine. It was like she was going to tryout right along with him, she was that excited. Maybe she felt it was her last shot at stardom. That if she couldn't make it in show business herself because of all the unfair obstacles life threw in her path, then maybe her only child would make it—and that would be just as gratifying. Eddie didn't know why she seemed so happy, so thrilled. All he knew was that he felt closer to his mother that night than ever before. It was grand—while it lasted.

The place was buzzing with excitement as over two hundred boys and their stage-mothers crammed the Gusman Center lobby that hot June day. A majority of them looked Hispanic, although there were a few gringos, blacks, and Asians scattered in the crowd.

Most of the boys wore T-shirts with sweat pants or shorts. Some even wore tights. The sissy ones, Eddie thought. Not him, though. He looked *bad* and he knew it. Tight jeans, shredded in all the right places, hugged his shapely, round ass. Tired old motorcycle boots from the thrift store gave him that dangerous air of a young Brando in one of those awful biker flicks. A black bandanna wrapped around his forehead kept his long, lustrous mane of auburn hair off his bad boy face. And the *pièce de résistance*: no T-shirt. Instead, he wore a black, leather jacket that one of his stepfathers had left behind, to cover the nakedness of his smooth, slender torso. *Bad*!

All the boys had numbers pinned to their shirts, Eddie to his jacket. He was number sixty-nine. An effeminate little man was handing out printed sheets of paper to the boys. When he came to Eddie, his beady eyes lingered on the boy's ass after giving him his copy.

Eddie and Maria quickly devoured the sheet, as did everyone else in the lobby. It read:

"Los Muchachos Rules…One, to be in Los Muchachos, a boy must be at least twelve years of age, good-looking, and speak fluent Spanish. Two, a Muchacho must be a talented singer and dancer, dedicated to performing. Three, Muchachos must be healthy, for they rehearse all the time when they're not performing; they must study hard and get good grades—a private tutor goes along on the tour so that the boys can keep up with their classes; they must not have bad habits, like cigarette-smoking or taking drugs; and they must get along well with others. Four, a member of Los Muchachos must *leave* the group before his sixteenth birthday, or if his singing voice changes, or he gets too tall."

They then read the history of Los Muchachos:

In 1979, Luis Miguel Martinez, an ex-dancer himself, got the idea to form a singing & dancing group that would perform in Spanish to audiences in Puerto Rico. He had no idea that MUCHACHOMANIA would soon sweep over the world when he recruited the original five talented boys. They worked incredibly hard on weekends and after school every single day. After long hours of repeating lyrics and dance steps, the boys began appearing in public on weekends. They'd perform to prerecorded music, so they didn't have to learn to play any instruments. In a year's time, the five dark-haired boys, dressed in identical outfits, became so popular that they began to travel—not only around their native Puerto Rico, but all over Latin America, performing for a growing multitude of fans. Then in 1981, Los Muchachos invaded America much like The Beatles did before them, making millions of new screaming, young fans. Nine years and thirteen different boys later, Los Muchachos are a hit all over the world, where many of their chart-topping albums have gone gold and platinum. They tour year round, have starred in two hit movies in Latin America, and their weekly TV show out of Puerto Rico is seen all over the globe. And the legend continues—*with you.*"

A nervous Eddie waited a couple of hours, behind the closed lobby doors, for the first three groups of twenty boys to audition. Now, it was finally his turn to take the stage. But he was with nineteen other boys. They stood shoulder to shoulder, upstage, filling the length of the platform. Numbers sixty-one thru sixty-eight were to Eddie's right, and numbers seventy through eighty were to his left.

Down center, on the apron facing them, stood the man. Above him, the tiny specks of light on the high ceiling, over the house, looked like stars in the night sky. Except for a mysterious boy in the darkness of the third row, this man seemed to be the only one who would be watching their audition. Eddie felt relieved at that. He really didn't know what to expect. Upon seeing over four hundred people waiting in the lobby, he was struck by the dreadful fear that they would all be sitting in the auditorium, evaluating his audition. That had sent a cold chill down his spine that almost made him wet his pants. Now, as he looked out into the empty house, he felt relieved. It wouldn't be that bad after all.

"Welcome, gentlemen," said the man with a thick Spanish accent. "I am Luis Miguel Martinez. I'm the creator, manager, producer, and choreographer of Los Muchachos." He spoke in a no-nonsense tone that filled Eddie with fear again.

Luis Miguel was a tall, muscular man with a slim dancer's build and long brown hair that he wore in a ponytail. He was slightly effeminate, yet came across exceedingly assertive and domineering, like a gay drill sergeant. He wore no shirt—just black tights and dance shoes—showing off the well-defined pectorals, biceps, and triceps hidden underneath a forest of thick body hair. Though quite handsome, he looked ragged, with dark circles under his eyes. Eyes which were an odd shade of green that seemed out of place against his dark complexion and Spanish features.

But wait, they were green contacts over black eyes, weren't they? Eddie couldn't tell. His gaze kept leaving the man's eyes and focusing on his bulging crotch. He didn't seem to be wearing any underwear, his big basket just protruded through his tights like two baseballs squeezed into a marble bag. His huge shaft appeared carefully positioned so as to come down his pants leg in front of his right thigh.

Eddie tried not to stare at it, but he couldn't help it. Just as he couldn't help the shifting in his jeans. He of course felt guilty, as he usually did when aroused by a man. Then a horrid thought slapped him in the face...

How the hell are you gonna dance with a fuckin' boner?!

Sweat was now pouring from every pore of his small body.

"For the first time ever, we are casting outside of Puerto Rico," Luis Miguel continued. "We are hoping that hiring a boy from America will broaden our appeal here in the States. Pedrito Rodriguez, who has been a Muchacho for four years now, will be turning sixteen next year, and maybe one of you will take his place."

They're only replacing one of them! thought Eddie, quite incensed.

He was suddenly struck by the harsh realization that there was no way he would be picked over two hundred other boys. He didn't have a snowball's chance in hell. He felt stupid for even being there and wanted desperately to go home. Yet the erection remained.

"Okay boys, spread out," directed Luis Miguel. "It's time for you young studs to show me what you've got! Make me excited!"

This sounded like a half-cheer and half-order, dripping with sexual overtones.

The man then walked the boys through complicated dance steps, repeating: "one, two, three, four, five, six, seven, eight," in time to a dance beat.

Eddie found the routine exceedingly easy. He had it down pat the first time through. Just as his insecurities were about to whisper in his ear that he was doing it all wrong, Eddie looked around at the other boys. It was the third and last time the choreographer was going over the steps, yet most of them were still tripping over their own feet. A powerful locomotive, with boxcars chock-full of self-confidence, suddenly struck him with a fury—bringing a cocky smile to his angelic face. It quickly became abundantly clear to him that he could dance circles around these boys. They looked like clumsy hippos in an old cartoon next to him. Maybe he *would* be picked after all!

The Muchachos hit, "Motorbike Daydreams" blasted through the boom box speakers at Luis Miguel's feet. The music didn't seem to help though, the other boys still appeared zombies next to Eddie. Not that they weren't good dancers; except for one hopeless case, they all had the steps down. It was their delivery that paled in comparison. He simply blew them off the stage.

A bright light, a magical presence, emanated from Eddie, filling the stage with a thermonuclear glow. His lithe, young body oozed of sensuality as it gyrated to the passionate Spanish rhythm. He appeared to fly through the air, flinging his limber limbs and landing effortlessly. He contorted his body like a seductive serpent, making every move his own. Especially the deep pelvic thrusts and a slow, erotic belly dance that was as hypnotic as watching a long, wiggling cobra coming out of a basket. He had become one with the music: a hot-blooded, Santeria priest from the islands—*his* islands—possessed by a hedonistic demon, and dancing around a campfire in a forbidden, carnal ritual; his pubescent loins hot, and his rock-hard six inches wanting to burst through his button fly.

Towards the end, some of the boys just stopped dancing to look at him go. But Eddie was in a trance of sorts, oblivious to everything but the music.

Luis Miguel turned off the tape, bringing Eddie back to reality. He suddenly became aware that everyone was staring at him. Some of the boys looked at him in awe, some in defeat, but most in envy. Their lips curling up to form a sneer.

Luis Miguel's eyes drank Eddie in, as if all he wanted to do was lick his sweaty body with a moist, hot tongue—tasting the burning droplets of sweat that trickled from his face onto his naked, velvety chest and pink, hard nipples. The intensity of Luis Miguel's stare made Eddie feel quite uncomfortable, if not confused.

"Thank you, men, that was..." Luis Miguel finally said, searching for the proper word, then finally giving up and settling for, "exhilarating." He took a deep breath and continued. "Number seventy-four and..." his stare was now ripping every stitch of clothes off Eddie's succulent body, "...oh yes, number sixty-nine. You two boys stay." His voice then turned cold and callous. "The rest of you may go. Thank you for coming."

In other words: fuck off; don't call us, we'll call you; welcome to the cruel cold world of real live showbiz, kiddies; and by the way, fuck off.

Disappointment engulfed the stage like flames in a dry forest. Eddie wanted to feel bad for the eighteen boys who were walking off, their dreams crushed. But he was too excited to feel much of anything except total euphoria.

Next came the singing part of the audition for number seventy-four—a gorgeous specimen of Latino boyhood, about fifteen—and number sixty-nine. Seventy-four sang a cappella. It was some obscure Spanish song that Eddie had never heard before. Eddie didn't much care for the song, but he did care for the tall boy's singing voice, not to mention the rest of him.

Eddie performed Michael Jackson's "Bad" along with the audio tape he'd brought. He miraculously recreated every dance move Jackson did in the video to the last detail. His clear, crisp voice filled the theatre—a delicate, yet loud, high flute with perfect-pitch—effortlessly drowning out Jackson's shrills. Midway through the song, in the dance break, he instinctively stripped off his jacket, somehow knowing Luis Miguel would enjoy it. His well-defined young torso glistened with perspiration.

That's right, he was *bad*!

Luis Miguel asked Eddie and Seventy-four to return the next day for a callback at noon, right before the matinee show. He tried to maintain a poker face, only telling Eddie that he was quite good for an amateur. But Eddie could see the man was impressed with his talent. Very impressed, as a matter of fact.

That night Eddie and his mother were too excited to sleep, so they stayed up talking all evening like friends at a slumber party. Again she didn't have a single drink all night long.

Morning finally came and Eddie took the number eleven bus, over the First Street bridge, to Downtown Miami. Maria had to work that afternoon, so Eddie had to go alone. He had of course promised to call her immediately if he was picked. Or, as she put it, *when* he was picked.

Eddie came in the backstage door just as he was told. The queeny little man with the beady eyes was there to let him in. He told Eddie that Mr. Martinez was conducting the callbacks in the main dressing room at the end of the hall. He then patted the boy's behind to start him walking in the right direction. Eddie felt violated by the man's touch, but was too nervous to think about it twice.

Around him, the place was a three-ring circus as people dashed past him preparing for the matinee show. He was quite overwhelmed by the sheer magnitude of the cavernous structure. He was also about to puke his brains out. As he got closer and closer to the dressing room door, his stomach sank deeper and deeper. It was the longest walk of his life and he was about to toss his cookies. Luckily, he saw the men's room out of the corner of his eye, making a run for it before making a mess on the floor. He got to the toilet just in time to deposit his breakfast.

As he knelt there hugging the porcelain bowl, he heard similar spewing noises coming from the next stall.

"Do you use your index finger or your middle one?" asked a young, impetuous voice with a Spanish accent.

Eddie stepped out of the stall to investigate its origin. The door to the adjacent stall was now cracked open, allowing Eddie to peer in. A slender boy about his age was kneeling next to the bowl. He wore only a short kimono that just barely covered his petite buttocks.

The pretty stranger repeated his odd question. Then, after wiping his mouth with his sleeve, he added, "I prefer the middle finger myself." With that, he stood with the grace of a ballet dancer and flushed the toilet with a flourish. He seemed to possess both male and female characteristics. This confused and intrigued Eddie simultaneously.

Eddie immediately recognized him, but couldn't quite place him. He looked *so* familiar: the shiny brown hair in a dutch-boy cut, the thick pouty lips, the contrast of his incandescent green eyes to his dark complexion, everything! "Do I know you?"

"Hi, Eddie," said the boy with a friendly smile. "I'm Juanie Santos from Los Muchachos."

Of course! He'd seen him a zillion times on TV. "How did you know my name?"

"I saw you audition yesterday. Damn, you were hot!"

Eddie was struck by a revelation of sorts. "You were the boy in the third row."

"That was me." His gaze had now wandered to Eddie's crotch. "I couldn't take my eyes off you. Nobody could."

"Thanks," said Eddie awkwardly, not knowing exactly how to take a compliment.

"I see you and me have something in common, man."

"What do you mean?"

"We make ourselves puke to stay skinny. It's the only way I can fit into those tight costumes."

Eddie had heard of girls doing that, but never boys. "I didn't make myself throw up!" he stated rather indignantly. "I'm just real nervous."

"Don't worry," said Juanie in a comforting tone. "Just do whatever Luis Miguel says and it'll be over before you know it. I usually help with initiation, but you're much too special to share. I'd rather wait till I can have you one on one, man." He then coyly winked at Eddie. "Bienvenido a Los Muchachos, Eddie."

Juanie gave him a quick peck on the lips and darted out of the men's room before Eddie could react.

He could not process the overwhelming influx of homoerotic data that deluged his mind at that moment. It was a multitude of emotions that were foreign to him.

My God! A boy just kissed me! Not just any boy, but Juanie Santos! Is he a faggot? I got a boner! Does that make me a faggot?! He had such a nice ass! Why did this have to happen now?! And what did he mean by "initiation"?!

Eddie looked like a zombie as he walked to the main dressing room. He was about to knock, when the door swung open and the boy who was number seventy-four from the audition ran out, pulling his pants up. A leather-clad Luis Miguel stood in the doorway holding a bullwhip.

"Damn it, boys, you know better than to leave the door unlocked!" A chorus of youthful voices begged his forgiveness from inside. "Well, he obviously didn't have what it takes to be a Muchacho." Luis Miguel looked at Eddie's stupefied face. "What the fuck are you looking at?! You're late!"

The muscle-bound man effortlessly pulled the boy into the room, quickly locking the door behind him. "Welcome to showbiz, *muchacho!*"

The horny groupies, the drugs and, oh yes, the hot nasty sex. It had been fun while it lasted—almost two years. Until that fateful night in 1990 when they were busted at Miami International Airport for drug trafficking. That was the downfall of Los Muchachos. But not of Eddie Pacheco. His star may have gone supernova, yet deep in his heart he knew it would someday shine once more.

Like the voice of God, if God were Latino, the announcer's booming baritone filled the auditorium, bringing Eddie back to reality. *"Y ahora damas y caballero, ex-Muchacho, Eddie Paaacheco!"*

The crowd roared when Eddie walked onto the stage. And when the follow-spot hit him, he knew that he was home again.

GAME FOR ANYTHING

As the son of a preacher man in Kansas, I led a sheltered youth. Alas, I was an eighteen-year-old virgin. That was to change when I went off to college in the early 80's.

In my freshman year, my goal in life was to become a coach's apprentice. I didn't care what sport. I just wanted to linger around the locker room as sweaty, young jocks disrobed and lathered their hard bodies. Man, I popped a woody just thinking about it.

I enrolled in the University's apprentice program and painstakingly worked towards my goal by getting good marks, volunteering for any and all sports activities, and maintaining a perfect attendance record. So when I was finally made an apprentice, I was ecstatic but not surprised. Hell, I deserved it!

That proud day, I stood shoulder to shoulder with my nine fellow apprentices as Dean Martinez assigned our commissions. What was it going to be? Football coach's apprentice? Basketball coach's apprentice? Wrestling coach's apprentice? Each one a prestigious assignment. "Library Apprentice," I repeated in sad disbelief as my colleagues snickered. I was crushed. It was like a police cadet expecting to make the SWAT Team but instead being stuck with a desk job. It sucked!

After my first week on the job, I realized that being Library Apprentice was even more boring than I had imagined. My duties varied: for a grueling half hour before and after classes, I "shhhed" people, returned books to their proper shelves, and straightened chairs. And my taskmaster was a peevish little man named Mr. Peepers, Master Librarian. The geeky dinosaur had run the library ever since the school opened thirty years back. Mr. Peepers was a stickler for rules; he was always on my case about something or other. "Chop, chop, Mister McIntyre," he would say, "there's no room for slackers on my watch. I run a shipshape ship, Mister."

With that he'd pat me on the behind and send me on my way. Sometimes his spidery hand would linger on my ass just a tad too long. This confused the hell out of me. Yes, it made me cringe. But surprisingly enough, it also gave me a whopper of an erection for some odd reason. Thinking about it gave me a headache, so I didn't.

Things began to get really strange my second week on the job when Mr. Peepers ordered me to straighten out his private reference section in the basement.

"The basement?!" I protested. I didn't even know the library *had* a basement. I pleaded with him for a good five minutes—telling him that I was afraid of the dark, not to mention spiders and other bugs that hide in dark, damp basements, just waiting to jump out at scared college boys. This was to no avail.

"Stop sniveling like a baby, Mister McIntyre!" he barked. "Go perform your task or I shall have to discipline you!"

This sent chills down my spine. He was a dark and sinister man and I didn't even want to think about how he would discipline me. I went down.

The secret stairway that led to the basement was dark and scary. The door creaked as I opened it to go in. My knees shook as I felt along the wall for the light switch. Every horror movie I had ever seen flooded my mind. I was expecting a werewolf or a mutant to grab my arm, savagely ripping it from its socket. I breathed a sigh of relief when I found the switch.

After saying a small prayer, I turned on the lights. But there were no monsters here—just books. The small room was chock-full of books. The walls were made of bookcases that reached all the way to the ceiling. I was pleasantly surprised. The room was not at all scary. On the contrary, it was downright cozy—like an old den. I plopped down on the black leather couch in the center of the room and looked around me. This wasn't going to be so bad after all.

A large book on the coffee table suddenly caught my eye. I leaned forward to get a better look. It had a most curious title, "Homosexuality: A Straight Man's Guide To Man To Man Coitis." Intriguing! "Fully Illustrated," it read in big letters on the bottom. Well, I couldn't stop myself, I just had to pick it up. My penis tingled at the thought of naked studs having sex with one another. My big blue eyes became even bigger as I excitedly opened the front cover. But nothing prepared me for what I found on the first page. Two well-toned college boys were playing leapfrog...naked. Only they were *so* close to each other that it looked like one of the boy's dicks was going up the other boy's butt. But that can't be, I thought. *What are they doing?!* My throbbing penis was so hard that I thought it was going to burst right through my pants.

A noise suddenly startled me, making me drop the book. I looked around the room, but there was no one there. Yet I felt like I was being watched for some reason. It was almost creepy. However, my lusty desire to see more of the book greatly outweighed my puerile fears. I quickly picked it up again. The bogus book-jacket had fallen off on the floor, revealing the book's salacious, real cover. I was dumbfounded. Five varsity boys stood over a brunette boy who was on all fours like a dog. They were peeing on him. The book's real title was: "Dutch Boy Golden Showers." I quickly devoured the book, furiously leafing through page after page of cute college boys engaging in activities I never even dreamed were possible. They were kissing, sucking, pissing on each other. They were even doing what my best friend Timmy used to call "corn-holing." Until I actually saw it in the book, I thought he was just making it up. But there it was in full color: "corn-holing." I began to tremble and grunt then, experiencing a huge orgasm in my trousers. That's when I heard Mr. Peepers coming down the stairs.

"Mister McIntyre, are you all right?" he queried with his high-pitched, whiny voice.

I utterly panicked, kicking the book-jacket under the couch and hiding the book under my shirt. The door creaked and I looked up.

There stood Mr. Peepers, staring at me quizzically. "Mister McIntyre, what is going on in here?" he demanded to know.

"Nothing, sir," I uttered.

"I could have sworn I heard guttural sounds emanating from down here."

"It's my stomach, sir," said I with a straight face. "I didn't have lunch."

He cocked an eyebrow, studying me for what seemed an agonizing hour. He then said, "Come boy, I'm closing up."

"Yes, sir," I blurted out. I carefully crossed my arms so that the book wouldn't fall out and stood up. "Are you cold, Mister McIntyre?"

Again I panicked. "Bye, Mr. Peepers," I said as I ran out the room and up the stairs, clutching the book to my stomach ever so tightly. "See ya tomorrow." I didn't stop running until I got to my dorm room.

I couldn't very well take a dirty book into my room. My homophobic roommate was always snooping through all my stuff. Therefore, I went to my Cousin Timmy's house. Timmy, who was my age, lived off-campus with my uncle—another Baptist preacher man. Timmy and his fraternal twin sister Tammy were just as sheltered as I was. We were three curious, freshman virgins in heat.

Luckily, Uncle Bill went out of town quite a lot, leaving the twins home alone. We did all kinds of naughty things then. We smoked cigarettes, watched R-rated movies on the betamax player, and hung around in our underpants. It had become our own little Sodom and Gomorrah. It was the perfect place to keep the book until I could somehow sneak it back into the library.

Timmy, Tammy, and I sat transfixed as I slowly flipped through the book. Timmy was shirtless as usual. His long blond locks drooping over his hazel eyes and upturned nose, his bronzed skin glistening with boy-sweat. I had always lusted for him. He was nonchalantly grabbing himself through his shorts.

Tammy, being the tomboy that she was, was likewise shirtless. The spitting image of her big brother, she looked more like a pretty boy than a girl. From the moment I opened the book, her hand never left her crotch area. They were both aroused beyond belief. This turned me on even more.

"This is so fucking hot, Justin!" Timmy exclaimed. "I don't believe you got this in the gosh darn library."

"All I can ever find there is 'Little House on the Prairie' books," Tammy bitched. "I like this better. Although, I wish there were girls in it too."

Timmy shocked us all by taking out a marijuana cigarette from his underwear drawer. He had gotten if from one of the boys that he tutored, in lieu of payment. We had never seen a marijuana cigarette, so Tammy and I literally gasped in astonishment.

Timmy dared us to smoke the "joint" with him. I never even considered doing drugs; however, I was so excited from the dirty book, that I threw caution to the wind. As for Tammy, she was a follower and usually did what her brother told her to do.

So Timmy lit the cannabis stick, and we passed it around like we had seen in movies. What we didn't know at the time was that Timmy's student had spiked the marijuana cigarette with something called Angel Dust. Before long, we had lost all sense of decorum.

Timmy stood to remove his shorts. His pretty dick was hard as a rock, with blond pubic hair all around. "Let's try some of the stuff in the book," he said eagerly.

I didn't need to be asked twice. I was out of my clothes in the blink of an eye. My penis was hard too. It was a lot smaller than Timmy's, but much fatter. Tammy quickly undressed as well. She also had blond hair down there, and I could actually see the wetness between her legs. I saw Timmy drop to his knees, then I felt an unbelievable warmth on my penis. The sight of Timmy taking me into his wet, luscious mouth was almost enough to knock me over. Tammy soon joined him, as they shared my penis in their hot mouths. I just had to giggle as I looked down at the book: it was as if page 107 had come to life, we were copying every move.

Tammy removed her pink lips from my penis to turn the page. "Hey, let's do this now," she said like a kid at Disneyland who wants to go on another ride. I too dropped to my knees to recreate the photo in the book. We embraced in a circle and joined our three tongues in the middle, licking, sucking, inviting one another's mouths. I had always longed to kiss Timmy, so I was in hog heaven, to say the least.

After several passionate moments, Timmy broke off to turn the page. "This one looks like even more fun," he said with a mischievous grin.

"Fuck yeah," I cried out, cursing for the first time in my eighteen years. And it felt great! Like a volcano with Tourette's, the dirty words began to erupt out of me: "Shit, fuck, pussy, cock! Mother Fuckin' Titty Suckin' Two Balled Bitch!" I was free!

Timmy lay on his side on the wooden floor. Tammy and I followed suit, forming a brand new circle. Timmy began to hungrily lap up his sister's pussy, while she sucked on my hard cock like a lollipop. I was beaming as I held Timmy's hard dick in my hand. It was throbbing in time to my heart. I felt wetness on my chin and noticed I was shamelessly drooling at this succulent sight.

"Suck it, Justin," said Timmy. "Yeah, suck it good, man." He then went back to eating out his sister.

And I did just that. I sucked it *good*. My fledgling taste buds came to life with this new, exotic savor: tangy, like sweat, with just a hint of piss. It was delicious. I was lost in a world of erotic madness and lovely sins of the flesh. As my hands caressed Timmy's silky thighs and plump buttocks, my skinny body convulsed yet another time; I had lost count after my third raging orgasm. I didn't think it could possibly get any better. But it did.

"Who wants to cornhole?" Timmy keenly asked, turning the page. Three pretty blond college boys were engaged in three-way penetration.

"But I have a pussy," Tammy whined.

"So we'll change it a little, that's all," Timmy assured her.

By that point I was game for anything. Tammy lay on her back with her legs over her brother's shoulders. Timmy then placed the head of his hard dick into his sister's moist pussy. "Not so hard this time, Timmy," she requested. "You hurt me last time."

They had done this before!

I couldn't believe it. No wonder they were so damn close. Timmy thrust his dick hard into his sister. A muffled scream escaped her, but I wasn't sure if it was from pain or pleasure.

"Come on, Justin," Timmy egged on, "corn-hole me." He fell on his sister, still fiercely humping her. "Spit into my asshole first like the guy in the book."

I knelt over him, releasing my spittle into his pink boy-pussy. Just then, I was struck with a sudden hankering to taste it. So I did just that. I lapped it up. Tasted better than his dick. Then I put my boner to his asshole and plunged it in hard, just like he had done to his poor sister.

Timmy screamed so loudly that I thought the whole block was going to come running. He begged me to take it out, writhing beneath me, trying to push me off him. But animal instinct took over; I was determined not to stop till I had finished. I mounted him, my hips furiously thrusting hard into him like dogs fucking. Timmy's pain was unbearable at first, then as he gave in and eased into it, I could actually feel his ass loosening up. I felt Timmy quaver under me as he came inside his sister, who in turn was having multiple orgasms. I shot yet another load before releasing Timmy.

We lay speechless on the floor, catching our breaths, looking as if we had just run a marathon.

But there was more to come. Timmy quickly got his second wind. He jumped to his feet and recreated the most daring tableaux of them all. He stood over Tammy and me, releasing his urine flux on us. We were both too stunned to react. Instead we just lay there and bathed in his piss.

I couldn't sleep at all that night. I knew I had fallen in love with Timmy—and that scared the shit out of me. I didn't want to be a faggot. But my biggest concern was how I was going to sneak that book back into the library basement.

The next morning, I hid the book in my book bag and waited for my accomplice, Timmy, to show up. He was going to create a diversion with Mr. Peepers while I slipped downstairs and replaced the book. We had seen something similar on "Hogan's Heroes."

Timmy showed up right on cue, faking an asthma attack. He was chewing up the scenery a little, but Peepers seemed to buy it. As he ran to Timmy's aid, I smoothly prowled into the basement. I ran straight for the couch and looked for the book jacket I had kicked underneath. But it wasn't there! Shit, where could it have gone? I was about to panic when I had a brainstorm. I would borrow a jacket from another book. Peepers would never know the difference. I ran to the bookcase and grabbed the first book I saw: "How To Train Your Pet." That would do. I removed its jacket and was about to breathe a sigh of relief, when I saw the book's true cover and title: "Pussyboys and their Masters." I couldn't believe it. I grabbed another book at random and removed its jacket. This one was called: "Dungeon Butt-fuck Jamboree." In a frenzy, I looked through book after book. They were *all* S&M porno! There was one big, black book—without a jacket—that stood out: it looked fake. I went for it, but it was wedged in the other books. I pulled on it with all my might until it finally budged. Only it pulled down like a lever, making the bookcase suddenly open to reveal a secret room. I was numb by then. Like some bimbo heroine in a bad "B" movie, I stepped into the mysterious room. It was a dungeon! A dungeon right underneath my picture-book college, filled with every torture device imaginable. "Welcome, Justin," said a familiar voice from the darkness.

I jumped out of my skin, losing control of my bladder.

He then added matter-of-factly, "We've been expecting you."

My eyes adjusted to the light and I could now see who it was. Dean Martinez was chained buck naked to the wall. I turned to run but Peepers was blocking the way. He was dressed all in leather and was holding a whip. He was also holding Timmy in a choke-hold. "Your diversion attempt was futile," Peepers stated smugly. "You've been very naughty. I'm going to have to discipline you both."

"I'm afraid you're going to be late for class today, boys," Martinez added. "But don't worry. I'll write you a note."

"Shut up! Slaves should be seen and not heard!" Peepers screamed at Martinez.

"Sorry, Master," Martinez wailed, now reduced to a subservient child. The Master cracked his bullwhip and threw Timmy and me into the dungeon. Our lives would never be the same again.

Thirty years later, the college still stands, the library still stands, even the secret dungeon still stands. Mr. Peepers, however, wasn't so lucky. He passed away in a freak gerbil accident. Martinez is a congressman now, Tammy is a big ol' lesbian truck driver, and Timmy wound up my longtime companion.

As for me, I took over Mr. Peeper's shipshape ship. I became the college librarian.

Shhh!

###

PJ Dominicis lives in South Florida and is currently working on other writing projects. His debut novel, "Depraved Blood: A Young Bloodsucker Vampire Tale," has been well received by critics and readers alike.

Printed in Great Britain
by Amazon